Amanda Faber
and
The Soldiers' Arts Academy
presents

SOLDIER ON
by Jonathan Lewis

directed by Jonathan Lewis

CAST

Nicholas Clarke	Jacko, Donny
Thomas Craig	Len
Sarah Jane Davis	Tanya, Sonja
Stephanie Greenwood	Ensemble
Mark Griffin	Rickshaw
Max Hamilton-Mackenzie	TC
Dean Helliwell	Understudy/Deputy SM
Rekha John-Cheriyan	Maggie
Drew Johnson	Ensemble
Shaun Johnson	Flaps
Tom Leigh	Understudy/Deputy SM
Cassidy Little	Woody
Steve Morgan	Hoarse
Lizzie Mounter	Beth
Ellie Nunn	Sophie
Robert Portal	Tom
Mike Prior	James/Cameron/Jenny/Darren
David Solomon	Harry
Philip Spencer	Understudy/Deputy SM
Hayley Thompson	Trees
Zoe Zak	Sal, Paula

CREATIVES AND PRODUCTION

Writer/Director	Jonathan Lewis
Producer	Amanda Faber
Assistant Director/ Choreographer	Lily Howkins
Fight Captain	Lizzie Mounter
Assistant Director	Andy Room
Associate Producer	Jessica Andrews
Company Stage Manager	Kate Thackeray
Lighting Designer	Mark Dymock
Composer/Sound Designer	Adam Gerber
Musical Director	Oli George Rew
Costume Designer, Head of Wardrobe, Make-up Artist and Props Manager	Sophie Savage
Video Technician	Simon Nicholas
Projection Designer	Harry Parker
Photographers	Amanda Searle, Harry Burton, Rupert Frere (Schmooly)
Film Makers	Neil Davies, Alex Dando
Production Manager	Seb Cannings
Company Advisor	Nick Shatford
Press	Iain McCallum, Anna Arthur, Kaija Larke
Marketing	Roman Baca
Assistant Producers	Claire Ackling, Freddie Lynch, Samara Smith, Claire Wesley, Helena Westerman, Rose Wetherby
Production Assistants	Emily Carter, Kate-Lois Elliott, Madeleine Kasson, Martha Reed
Consulting	Dewynters Marketing and Advertising Consultants
Accountants	Mark Hopkins WMYOB and Blinkhorns

SOLDIERS' ARTS ACADEMY CIC

The Soldiers' Arts Academy provides a platform for the arts for serving and ex-service personnel – some of whom have been injured mentally and/or physically during their time in service. It enables them to recover, to train in the arts including performance skills and to transition back into work either in the performing arts or outside. It aims for them to develop opportunities which will enable them to fulfil their artistic potential and to find work. Covering all aspects of the arts including theatre, film, dance, art, poetry and music, the SAA works in partnership with the Royal Foundation to run workshops with military personnel. It also offers educational workshops nationwide in schools and colleges.

soldiersartsacademy.com

Above: photo: Amanda Searle; make-up: James Anda

Left: 'Company in Rehearsal', drawing by Harry Parker.

NICHOLAS CLARKE | **JACKO/DONNY**

Nicholas is delighted to be reprising the roles of Jacko and Donny in *Soldier On* after the earlier sell-out tour. Theatre includes: *Afterbirth* (Park Theatre); *In/Out (a feeling)* (Hope Theatre); *Hazard* (Bush Theatre, Boom festival); *It Never Ends* (theatre 503); *All Alone* (Drayton Arms Theatre); *Miss Julie* (Bussey Building); *Meat* (Albany); *Taken In* (Tristan Bates Theatre). Film/Series includes: *Are We Dead Yet?* and *Bronzed*. Twitter @**Nick_Clarke99**

THOMAS CRAIG | **LEN**

Tom trained at ALRA between 1985-88 and this year celebrated 30 years in the profession. He was in Jonathan Lewis's first play *Our Boys* and also a member of the original cast at The Cockpit Theatre. Jonathan and Tom also collaborated on *The Club* at The Old Red Lion and Edinburgh Festival with Tom producing and performing, while Jonathan directed. As well as this being their third play together, they also appeared in *Soldier Soldier* together, where Jonathan was Tom's Company Sgt Major. Theatre includes: *Soldier On* (Playground Theatre and UK Tour); *The Armour* (The Langham Hotel); *Shang a Lang* (Kings Head Theatre); *The Kitchen* and *Disappeared* (The Royal Court). Film includes: *Hyena* (Director: Gerard Johnson); *The Navigators* (Ken Loach). Television includes: *Murdoch Mysteries*, two and a half years on *Coronation Street*, six seasons of *Where The Heart Is*, final season of *Soldier Soldier* and *Madson* for the BBC. Tom's first TV credit was as a regular on *The Paradise Club* back in the 80's!

SARAH JANE DAVIS | **TANYA / SONJA**

Sarah was a Lance Corporal in 3 regiment Army Air Corps, and did active service in Iraq in 2003 on the frontline supporting the joint helicopter force in and around Basra, securing landing points and providing aid drops for the civilians. She also did a stint in the military Provost Guard Service, and since leaving the services has done reserves and volunteers for the Army cadet force as an adult instructor. Sarah has been doing weapon safety on film sets, with experience in special effects and explosives. She has been an extra, a model, and also does private security as well as bringing up her two children. Supporting this great organisation is something close to her heart, with friends being lost to mental illness and PTSD. Sarah has a strong belief that only with greater awareness and understanding from more people, this will gain support, and the wider veteran community can gain a better quality of life. Television work, special effects and Armourer work includes: *Casual*

Vacancy (BBC); *Our World War* (BBC); *Drift Car Challenge* (Sky Active Channel); *Broadchurch, How I Live Now, Montana, He Who Dares, The Carrier, Welcome to Curiosity. Twitter* **@Sarah79barnett**

STEPHANIE GREENWOOD | **ENSEMBLE**

Stephanie is a London based actress and writer. She graduated from Dartmouth College (USA) with a degree in theatre and politics. She comes to *Soldier On* after having written and performed her one woman show *It's Beautiful, Over There* at the Camden Fringe. Theatre includes: *It's Beautiful Over There* (Upstairs at the Gatehouse); *Soldier On* (Playground Theatre and UK Tour); *The Brand* (Bunker Theatre); *Blue Stockings* (Bentley Theatre). Twitter **@stephmgreenwood**

MARK GRIFFIN | **RICKSHAW**

Mark's first acting role came when he moved to Los Angeles and was cast as the lead role in the Disney TV series *Action Man*. He stayed in L.A. for the next fourteen years, working alongside such luminaries as Eddie Murphy, Diane Keaton, Jeff Daniels, Anna Faris, Mark Harman and Jean-Claude Van Damme to name a few, as well as having recurring roles on CBS's *Days of Our Lives* and guest starring in *Curb Your Enthusiasm, NCIS, I Did Not Know That, The Smoke, Doctor Who,* and the role of Brandon Vickers in the finale of HBO's *Strike Back.* UK theatre includes: *Touching The Blue, Edinburgh Fringe, A Second of Pleasure, Those The River Keeps,* Pinter's *Betrayal, The Merchant of Venice, Closer, The Good Doctor, Apologia* (all at the Bridge Theatre in Richmond); *Bluebird* and *Wastwater* (The Tabard); *The Two Faces of Agent Lacey* (Above The Arts, Leicester Square); *Soldier On* (Playground Theatre and UK Tour). Film includes: *Doctor Dolittle II, Daddy Day Care, The Hard Corps Dragons of Camelot, I Am Vengeance, Bromley Boys, Jurassic World: Fallen Kingdom.* Twitter **@themarkgriffin**

MAX HAMILTON-MACKENZIE | **TC**

Max Hamilton-Mackenzie is an actor who served in the Royal Green Jackets. His first acting role was in the Film *Strelyayushchiya Angely* alongside Rupert Everett filmed in Moscow in 1992. Max has worked in the music industry as well as a photojournalist and continues to compose music. Theatre includes: *Soldier On* (Playground Theatre and UK Tour) *Richard III* (RSC Swan Theatre, Leicester Square Theatre). Films include: *Bond Skyfall, A Little Chaos, Star Wars: Rogue One, Dracula Untold.* More info at **www.maxhamilton.co.uk**

REKHA JOHN-CHERIYAN | **MAGGIE**

Rekha John-Cheriyan is an actor and writer. She comes to *Soldier On* in the West End fresh from a run at Derby Theatre in *Beyond Shame*. Rekha is also a passionate supporter of new writing and has worked on productions at Jermyn Street, New Diorama, The Vaults and Park Theatre. She has also been part of the Wandsworth Fringe. As a writer, her work has been well-received by audiences at Tristan Bates, The Bunker and the Lion & Unicorn. She is working on a number of new project, while juggling regular corporate and charity work such as role-play and reading for *Talking Newspaper*. Theatre includes: *Beyond Shame* (Derby Theatre); *Much Ado About Nothing* (Waterloo East); *Fats and Tanya* (The Etcetera); *The Deranged Marriage* (UK Tour). Film includes: *Tomb Raider* (Warner Bros/Raider Productions). Twitter **@cheryoncake**

DEAN HELLIWELL | **UNDERSTUDY / DEPUTY SM**

Dean served with the Duke of Lancaster's infantry Regiment. He moved to London earlier this year to pursue a career as a professional actor and he is currently training at city Lit with his friend and mentor Gary Grant. Through his training, Dean has realised that acting is what he was born to do. Gary also put him in touch with the Soldiers' Arts Academy where he is understudying a few characters and will be making his theatre debut as Len. Dean says: 'I am delighted and humbled to be a part of an organisation that has such amazing and talented individuals. It helps to promote and convey the message to other members of the military family, that the performing arts is a great way to help them heal and to integrate back into civilian life. There are lots of others in the room to help and support each other along the way'. Twitter **@DeanHelliwell**

TOM LEIGH | **UNDERSTUDY / DEPUTY SM**

Tom is an Ex-Royal Marines Commando who surprised everyone with a transition to acting after leaving the military in 2015, due to suffering an injury on operations in Afghanistan. Using his military experiences to drive his work ethic and performance and to give him a unique viewpoint, he trained with Richard Stride from the Groundlings Theatre, Portsmouth. Tom started performing as often as possible with the desire to show other veterans that they can be successful in their 'second life'. Recent credits include: *My Fair Lady* (Several); *Coriolanus*, (Aufidius); *Pink Triangle* (Claudio); *No Name* (Prince Charming) and several TV/Film projects.

PHILIP SPENCER | **UNDERSTUDY**

Phil has served in the Royal Marines for 10 years and has deployed on multiple operational tours across the globe. Most recently, he has been training recruits at the Commando School of Excellence but due to old injuries sustained in Afghanistan is now facing medical discharge. This has reignited Phil's lost love for the arts and has set him on his journey which has led to the Soldiers' Arts Academy. Phil has a keen interest in writing and acting and is excited to be supporting the production of *Soldier On*.

DREW JOHNSON | **ENSEMBLE**

Drew comes from a long line of Royal Marines, which is why he joined the British Army. He served in various roles and in many countries with the Army for over fifteen years, eventually ending up as a helicopter pilot in the Army Air Corps. Having been diagnosed with PTSD, stemming from operational tours, Drew was medically discharged and faced uncertainty. So he trained at the Academy of Live and Recorded Arts, and is now living his 'second life' as an actor. Theatre includes: *Closer, Ivanov, 4.48 Psychosis, Merchant of Venice, True Care – Prepare, Great Expectations, Suicide Bomb* (ALRA); *Cam Girl* (Arden Theatre). Television includes: *The Amazing Race* (CBS). Twitter **@drewjohnsonact**

SHAUN JOHNSON | **FLAPS**

Former Soldier – fought baddies on several tours of duty and looked pretty sitting on ceremonial horses for The Queen. Shaun has appeared on television, radio, and in national newspapers talking about his own 'mind-frag' challenges. He is in production with Dai4Films making a TV documentary highlighting the many transitional difficulties veterans face after leaving the military family. In *Soldier On* he is honoured to be carrying the flag on behalf of the Royal Regiment of Artillery. Recent Theatre includes: *Soldier On* (The Playground Theatre and UK Tour); *Hamlet* (Shakespeare's Globe); *Twelfth Night* (Leicester Square Theatre); *Richard III* (RSC Swan Theatre and Leicester Square Theatre); *The Comedy of Errors* (The Lansburgh Theatre, Washington DC). Shaun will appear at The Shakespeare's Globe Sam Wannamaker Playhouse Sunday 11th November to mark the Centenary of the Great War. Twitter **@Shaun5195**

CASSIDY LITTLE | **WOODY**

As a Royal Marine Commander, Cassidy lost a leg in Afghanistan in 2011. Within three months of recovery, he was part of The Bravo 22 Company playing the lead role of Charlie in *The Two Worlds of Charlie F.* by Owen Sheers. Cassidy won the nation's hearts when he was awarded the first BBC's Peoples' Strictly (for Comic Relief). Theatre includes: *The Two Worlds of Charlie F* (Theatre Royal Haymarket); *Explosion* (Compania de Flamenco); *The Trial of Jane Fonda* (The Park) and *Soldier On* (Playground Theatre and UK Tour). Television includes: *Doctors, Holby City, Rated* (Film and Game Review show); *Coronation Street, Strictly Come Dancing, Christmas Day Special.* Twitter @**Cassidy_1664**

STEVE MORGAN | **HOARSE**

Steve joined the army as a young man and soon left to pursue a life in the USA. Whilst there he attended the Chris Wilson School of Acting in Houston, Texas. He returned to the UK, joined the reserves and is still serving. After a tour in Afghanistan he joined the Soldiers' Arts Academy. Theatre includes: *Annie Get Your Gun, Fiddler on the Roof* (Chris Wilson School of Acting); *Henry V* (The Old Vic Tunnels); *Richard III* (RSC Swan Theatre, Leicester Square Theatre); *Soldier On* (Playground Theatre and UK Tour).

LIZZIE MOUNTER | **BETH**

Lizzie Mounter graduated from RADA. She has since co-formed the theatre company Mugshot Theatre, co-producing and performing in their debut play *Sisterbound* at the Camden Fringe last year. Theatre includes: *Much Ado About Nothing* and *The Importance of Being Earnest* (RADA Studios-Cunard Company); *Soldier On Tour* (Playground Theatre and UK Tour); *Who Cares* (The Lowry); *Sisterbound* (Hen & Chickens Theatre); *Hamlet* (Cockpit Theatre). Short film includes: *Withheld* (Blue Cedar Films); *The Effect* (Met Film School).

ELLIE NUNN | **SOPHIE**

Ellie Nunn most recently appeared as Minnie Gasgoine in *The Daughter in Law* at The Arcola Theatre, a role she will reprise when the show returns in January 2019. When no one will employ her she has been known to stage, devise and perform a series of entirely self-indulgent concerts called *Ellie Nunn Sings Songs at People.*

Theatre includes: *Soldier On* (Playground Theatre and UK Tour); *When Midnight Strikes* (The Drayton Arms); *Honk!* (The Union Theatre); *Can't Stand Up For Falling Down* (Theatre N16); *Twelfth Night* for Grassroots (Leicester Square Theatre); *Desperate Measures* (Jermyn Street Theatre); *Gatsby* (Arts Theatre); *Shakespeare in Love* (Noel Coward Theatre); *Lady Windermere's Fan* (Kings Head Theatre/Ruby in the Dust) and Joanna Murray Smith's one woman show *Bombshells* (Jermyn Street Theatre/ Dippermouth). Film includes: *Chubby Funny* (Free Range Films/ Aim Image Productions); *Cracks* (Element Pictures/Studio Canal); *The Brief History and Untimely Death of George III* and *Guinea Pig* (Try Hard Films). Twitter **@ellienunn**

ROBERT PORTAL | **TOM**

Theatre includes: *The Rivals, The Venetian Twins, Love's Labours Lost* (RSC); *The Invention of Love, The Doctor's Dilemma* (NT); *Tom and Viv* (Almeida); *Noises Off, The 39 Steps, Calico, The Truth* (West End). Film includes: *Hurricane Tales From the Lodge, Goodbye Christopher Robin, Eat Local, The Ghost Writer, 6 Days, Meet Pursuit Delange, Mr Turner, Snow White-Winters War, Kids in Love, Welcome to the Punch, The Iron Lady, My Week With Marilyn, Mothers Milk, The King's Speech, In Your Dreams, Mrs Dalloway, Still Upper Lips.* Television includes: Grantchester, *Porters* (Series 2); *Death in Paradise, Collateral, Endeavour* (Series 5); *Birds of a Feather*—Christmas Special, *Royal Blues/Henry IX, The Rebel, Psychoville, In Love With Barbara, Ashes to Ashes, Rosemary and Thyme, The Great Belzoni, Distant Shores, Bye Bye Baby.*

MIKE PRIOR | **JAMES / CAMERON / JENNY/ DARREN**

Mike trained at the Guildford School of Acting, graduating in 2015. Before that he was a helicopter pilot in the British Army. Theatre includes: *Soldier On* (Playground Theatre and UK Tour); *Absent Friends* (Reading Between the Lines); *The Comedy of Errors* (Lansburgh Theatre, Washington D.C.) and *Hamlet* (Shakespeare's Globe. Short film includes: *Mercy* (TNT Films). Military Advisor credits include: *Our Boys* (Q Productions); *Journey's End* (RADA). Twitter **@mikedprior**

DAVID SOLOMON | **HARRY**

David trained at RADA. After several years in the business, he hung up his leotard and started training business people to express themselves. After 20 years of living a responsible life, he jumped at the chance of a comeback and fooled most of the people most of the time in the award winning, sell out run of *Soldier On*.

The transfer to The Other Palace was an irresistible opportunity to extend a much needed mid-life crisis. Theatre includes: *Soldier On* (The Playground Theatre and UK Tour); *King Lear* (Royal Shakespeare Company); *a part too small to remember in a play everyone forgot* (National Theatre); *Merchant of Venice* (Manchester Library Theatre); *Measure for Measure* (The Oxford Stage Company). Television includes: *Eastenders, The Politician's Wife* and *Love Hurts*. Twitter **@sunmoontraining**

HAYLEY THOMPSON | **TREES**

Hayley left school at sixteen and trained as a Jockey at the British Racing School Newmarket. She then moved on to join the Royal Army Medical Corps, and was described as an exemplary soldier, in both her medical training and physical training. She was awarded for her outstanding athletics contributions and was presented with the award for the best recruit at physical exercise.

Since then she has gone on to complete training in Midwifery, Psychology and Mental Health Nursing, finding her passion in caring for young children who have experienced severe trauma, and by helping to make a positive impact on their lives. Hayley first found her love of performing as a child, training in Ballet, Tap, Modern dance and gymnastics to a high standard. She has performed in theatre, TV and Film. Hayley feels honoured to be playing the role of Trees in the production of *Soldier On*. Hayley would like to thank Jonathan Lewis and Amanda Faber for this wonderful opportunity.

ZOE ZAK | **SAL/PAULA**

Zoe is a London based actress who has worked across stage, screen and radio. At the age of eight, she played the titular role of *Oliver* in the school play and, after taking the Method approach (pick-pocketing anyone who entered the family home), she decided this was the career for her. She went to The Brit School of Performing Arts and later continued her development with The Young Vic taking part in various projects and productions, including the American Opera, *Street Scene*, directed by John Fulljames. She has also trained and worked with The North Wall Theatre, Old Vic New Voices and The Actors Class. Theatre includes: *Pinch Punch* (The Old Vic); *Soldier On* (The Playground Theatre and UK Tour); *The Disintegration Loops* (*The North Wall*); *Foxfinder* (*Edinburgh Fringe*); *Hatton Garden Diamond Heist* (National Youth Theatre); *Housed* (The Old Vic); *Street Scene* (The Young Vic); *One Flew Over the Cuckoo's Nest* (Edinburgh Fringe); *Hamlet* and *Annie Get Your Gun* (The Young Vic). Television includes: *Doctors* (BBC). Voiceover includes: *Soy Luna* (Disney). Twitter: **@Zoe_Zak**

Above: Rekha John-Sheridan as Maggie and Thomas Craig as Len.
Below: company in rehearsal

Company in rehearsal

Above: Cassidy Little as Woody
Right: Shaun Johnson as Flaps

Above: Mark Griffin, Max Hamilton-Mackenzie,
Zoe Zak, Lizzie Mounter, Hayley Thompson, .

Below: the company.
Photographer: Harry Burton

'Airbridge'
Photographer, Rupert Frere

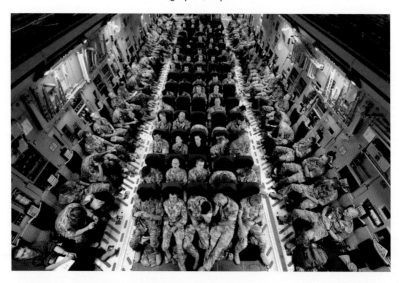

'Coming for a Bine'
Photographer, Rupert Frere

Creative Team

JONATHAN LEWIS | **WRITER / DIRECTOR**

.Jonathan has worked extensively as an actor, writer and director for over 20 years, and has won a number of awards for his work. His first play was *Our Boys* – which he also directed at the Soho Theatre, Derby Playhouse and at the Donmar Warehouse – for which he won the Writers' Guild Award for Best New Fringe Play, TAPS new Television Writer of the Year, and was nominated for the Lloyds Bank Playwright of the Year. *Our Boys* was revived in a major West End production in the Autumn of 2012, and was nominated for a number of awards including Best Revival and Best Acting Ensemble at the *Evening Standard* Awards as well as the *What's On Stage* Awards. He also wrote and directed *A Comedy of Arias* at The Pleasance, Edinburgh as part of a Pick of the Fringe season at the New Ambassadors Theatre in London's West End, as well as his own play *All Mouth* at the Menier Chocolate Factory. He has co-written and performs *I Found My Horn* which has played at theatres and festivals up and down the country (also Copenhagen, Lisbon, Abu Dhabi, New York, LA and at the Laguna Beach Playhouse). He also directed *The Club* by David Williamson and Chris England's hit shows, *Breakfast with Johnny Wilkinson* (Menier Chocolate Factory and Edinburgh Fringe) and *Twistorm* at the Park Theatre. He is currently working on a trilogy for the theatre entitled *Education, Education, Education*. Part one, called *A Level Playing Field,* premiered at the Jermyn Street Theatre in April 2015. Part two, *The Be All and End All,* premiered at York Theatre Royal in May 2018. **@Jonnyguylewis**

AMANDA FABER | **PRODUCER**

Amanda works as a producer,writer and director in film, television, theatre and dance. She founded The Soldiers' Arts Academy and The Charlie F Project (UK) Ltd. and was a director of *Combat Veteran Players* and *Shakespeare's Soldiers* (Soliloquy Pictures Ltd). For film her credits include: *How the Stage Saved a Soldier* (Soldiers' Arts Academy, 2017) and *The Covenant* (2017); *Jadoo* (2012) which premiered in official selection at the Berlin Film Festival 2013; *Resistance* (2011), nominated for the Cine Vision Award at the Munich Film Festival and for which Sharon Morgan won a Welsh BAFTA 2012 for Best Actress. Televison credits include: *Breaking the Silence, Guilty my Arse, The Race for Everest, Children with a Difference, Crooked Britain* and *Watchdog* (BBC). Theatre includes: *Richard III* (2017); *Twelfth Night* (2016). Dance includes: *Muster* (2015), *Traces of War,* and *Remember* (2017). **@amandafaber**

LILY HOWKINS | **ASSISTANT DIRECTOR / CHOREOGRAPHER**

Lily is resident choreographer for Theatre Sotto Voce, with whom she has been working on a new children's musical, *Behind Enchanted Windows*, developing the choreography through an R&D process at the Unicorn Theatre. Previous movement direction and choreography includes: *Our Boys* (PQA Venues); *Honk!* and *H. R. Haitch* (The Union Theatre); *Caste, Our American Cousin* (The Finborough Theatre); *By My Strength* (R&D with Brickdust Theatre); *The Tinderbox* (Charing Cross Theatre);*The Blues Brothers Summer Special* (The Hippodrome); *Ecstasies Within* (The Southbank Centre and Latitude Festival); *The Blues Brothers Xmas Special* (The Arts Theatre); *Murder In Whitechapel* (Tristan Bates Theatre); *Arnika* (The Bridewell Theatre); *Shirleymander* (The Playground Theatre); *Jack and The Beanstalk, Puss In Boots, Robin Hood* (Greenwich Theatre). Lily was the co-director and choreographer for the physical theatre piece *Hood!* (Edinburgh Fringe Sell-Out Award with Peculius Theatre) and has assistant directed for *Our Boys* and *Jack and The Beanstalk*. Last year she choreographed Buxton Opera House's pantomime *Sleeping Beauty*, and is looking forward to returning this year with *Dick Whittington*.

ANDY ROOM | **ASSISTANT DIRECTOR**

Andy is a theatre director and magician. Previous productions include *HONKk!* (Union Theatre), *Doctor Faustus* (St Paul's Church, Islington); *Into the Woods* and *The Twits* (ADC Theatre). As Assistant/ Associate, work includes the Olivier Award-nominated *Peter Pan Goes Wrong* (Apollo Theatre, West End); *The Comedy About a Bank Robbery* (Mischief Theatre); *This Much* (Soho Theatre); *The Tempest* (Iris Theatre) and the UK Premiere of Stiles and Drewe's *The Three Little Pigs* (UK Tour/ Palace Theatre, West End).

JESSICA ANDREWS | **ASSOCIATE PRODUCER**

Jessica attended Film School at NYFA and participated in the Royal Court Theatre's prestigious Young Writers' programme. Film work includes roles at Francis Ford Coppola's American Zoetrope, and with ABC and Academy nominated director, Peter Medak. In theatre Jessica has worked on Cameron Mackintosh's West End production of *Mary Poppins* and James Todd's *When Harry Met Sally* (Theatre Royal Haymarket). She's also worked in production on her own plays at the Tristan Bates, also *Picasso* at the Playground Theatre. Jessica is currently working as a Creative Producer on multimedia projects in the U.K and U.S.A.

KATE THACKERAY | **COMPANY STAGE MANAGER**

Kate trained at the Guildhall School of Music and Drama. Recent credits include: Stage Manager on Kathleen Turner's *Finding My Voice* (The Other Palace); Deputy Stage Manager on *Coraline* (The Barbican Centre for the Royal Opera House); Stage Manager on *Das Rhinegold, Mahler 8* and *Fidelio* for the London Philharmonic Orchestra at Royal Festival Hall. Company Stage Manager for the *Our House* (UK Tour); Stage Manager on *Romeo et Juliette* and *Die Walkure* at Grange Park Opera.

MARK DYMOCK | **LIGHTING DESIGNER**

Credits include: *Once* (regional premiere: New Wolsey and Queens); *Ken* (Terry Johnson, Pleasance); *Revenants* (Pleasance, Kenwright); *Loves Labours Lost* (GSC); *Dell Computers Gala (*Buenos Aires); *Rope* (Queens and New Wolsey); *Cathy* (Soho Theatre); *East* (Brighton Theatre Royal and Festival); *Sleeping Beauty, Aladdin* (Evolution); *Meena and the Masala Queens* (Rifco tour) *Northanger Abbey* (Bury St Edmunds Theatre Royal Tour); *Clybourne Park* (Regional premiere tour), *Return to the Forbidden Planet* (25th Anniversary tour); *Cathy* (Cardboard Citizens tour); *Betty Blue Eyes (*Regional premiere tour); Michael Morpurgo's *Butterfly Lion* (Kenwright, National Tour); *Snow White, Peter Pan, Wind in the Willows, James and the Giant Peach, Noises Off, Friend or Foe, The History Boys, The Hired Man,* (Mercury Theatre); *House and Garden, Alice in Wonderland, Peter Pan, Pinocchio, Arabian Nights, Treasure Island, Wind in the Willows* (Watermill); *Roll Over Beethoven, Don't Look Now* (OFFIE nominated for Best Lighting Design); *Return to the Forbidden Planet, Godspell, The Merchant of Venice, Can't Pay? Won't Pay!, They're Playing Our Song, Jack and the Beanstalk, Cinderella, Ladies Down Under, The Woman Who Cooked Her Husband* (Queens Theatre); *The Deranged Marriage, MummyJi Presents, Break The Floorboards and Happy Birthday Sunita* (Rifco and Watford Palace); *Walking the Chains* (Bristol Temple Meads Passenger Shed); *The Full Monty, Best Little Whorehouse in Texas, Oliver!,* (Bermuda City Hall); working with Willy Russell on *Educating Rita, Breezeblock Park* (Liverpool Playhouse); *Shirley Valentine* (Royal Court Liverpool); *Farm Boy, The Hired Man, Kissing Sid James* (New York E59). Twitter **@Scarletmark**

ADAM GERBER | **COMPOSER / SOUND DESIGNER**

Adam is a Conductor, Composer, and Musical Director in London working on projects in a variety of musical genres. Originally from Scotland, he trained under Paul Mealor and Chris Gray at The University of Aberdeen. Whilst in Scotland, Adam enjoyed working with companies such as The Citizens' Theatre and Scottish Opera and was a founder of The Marischal Chamber Orchestra touring both in the UK and Europe. Since moving to London, Adam has been involved in a breadth of theatrical output including musicals, plays, and immersive experiences creating work in some of the most exciting venues in the city and the regions. A sought-after educator, he has had the pleasure of guest lecturing at many of the top drama schools in the country with particular focus on acting through song. Adam is represented by Nick Quinn and Maeve Bolger at The Agency. For further information, visit **www.adamgerber.co.uk**

OLI GEORGE REW | **MUSICAL DIRECTOR**

Training: Mountview Academy of Theatre Arts (Musical Direction, Recipient of Help Musicians UK's Lesley Hayes Award) and University of Cambridge. Musical Directing and Musical Supervising credits include: *Give My Regards To Broadway* (Upstairs at the Gatehouse); *H.R.Haitch and Honk!* (Union Theatre); *Soldier On* (Playground Theatre and UK Tour); *Hot Lips and Cold War* (London Theatre Workshop); *Snow White and the Seven Dwarfs* and *Aladdin* (Theatre Royal Bath); *When Midnight Strikes* and *Birds of Paradise* (Drayton Arms Theatre); *Chicken Little, DinoStory* and *Song Writers' Showcase* (From Page to Stage Festival of New Musical Theatre, The Other Palace Studio); *Mary Stuart: The Musical* (Workshop, Mountview Catalyst Festival 2017); [*title of show*] (Waterloo East Theatre); *Busters* (Bernie Grant Arts Centre); *Cinderella, Jack and the Beanstalk* (The Maltings, Ely) and *Hello, Dolly!* (ADC Theatre, Cambridge). Assistant Musical Directing credits include: *Swallows and Amazons* (University Parks, Oxford); *On the Town* (University of Chichester); *Blondel* (Union Theatre); *Paper Hearts* (Edinburgh Fringe 2016); *Anne of Green Gables* (Unicorn Theatre); Undergraduate Musical Theatre Showcase 2015 (Phoenix Theatre) and First Lady Suite (Karamel Club). Cabaret credits include: *Roles I'll Never Play* (91 Brick Lane); *A Night at the Movies* (Phoenix Artist Club) and *West End Night Off* (Pizza Express Live, High Holborn). Future credits include: *Peter Pan* (Theatre Royal, Bath). Twitter **@OliRew1**

SOPHIE SAVAGE | **COSTUME DESIGNER, HEAD OF WARDROBE, MAKE-UP ARTIST, PROPS MANAGER**

After Sophie was medically discharged from the RAF, she was unsure what her next step would be and where life would take her. After many years of ups and downs and struggles trying to choose an enjoyable, positive and self satisfying career, Sophie is now a qualified award winning makeup artist and plans to take her make-up skills to the next level. Sophie covers a wide range and variety of work from theatre and weddings to TV, film and events. She worked in a major role on the UK tour and this production of of *Soldier On*.

SIMON NICHOLAS | **VIDEO TECHNICIAN**

Simon is co-founder of the award winning OVO Theatre Company. His passion is the creative integration of film and projection into productions: shows include *Romeo and Juliet, The New World Order, The Ladykillers, Betrayal, Chess, Return to the Forbidden Planet, Yes Prime Minister, The Merry Wives of Windsor, The History Boys, A Christmas Carol* and *Cats*. As a filmmaker, in 2017 he travelled to China to report on the work of Project Sunshine, a project that encourages poorer children in remote rural schools to improve their English through play and performance. He has just returned from filming their second visit.

HARRY PARKER | **SET & PROJECTION DESIGNER / ARTIST IN RESIDENCE**

Harry Parker was educated at Falmouth College of Art, University College London and the Royal Drawing School. He joined the British Army when he was twenty-three and served in Iraq in 2007 and Afghanistan in 2009 as a Captain. He is now a writer and artist and lives in London. His first novel, *Anatomy of a Soldier*, was published by Faber in 2016.

AMANDA SEARLE | **PHOTOGRAPHER**

Amanda Searle is a portrait and fashion photographer with a reputation for capturing iconic and moving images of people, including leading figures from the worlds of comedy, music, television, film and politics. Her commissions range from album covers and billboards to projects for Italian *Vogue*, English National Opera, the BBC, ITV and Channel 4, also the NHS and Charities such as Age UK and Variety Children's Charity. She has worked closely with the Soldiers' Arts Academy, producing a series of portraits of veterans whose lives have been impacted by their time in service.

HARRY BURTON | **PHOTOGRAPHER, ACTOR, DIRECTOR**

Harry trained as an actor at the Central School, and later as a director with BBC Television. He has acted and directed in theatre, television, film and radio for over thirty years. He directed Jonathan Lewis in the acclaimed one-man show *I Found My Horn*. At Dartington this summer, Harry played JS Bach in *The Great Passion*. He is currently acting in the World Premiere of *Sweet Lorraine*, by Gary Wilmot. Harry recently directed Mark Rylance in *Pinter's Art, Truth and Politics* at the Harold Pinter Theatre. Harry teaches at Drama Centre in London, and lectures on the work of Harold Pinter internationally. He directed the Channel 4 documentary, *Working With Pinter*. **harryburton@me.com**

RUPERT FRERE | **PHOTOGRAPHER, SCHMOOLY AGENCY**

Rupert is a serving British Army Photographer and company director of Schmooly. He became an Army Photographer in 2007 after transferring from 11EOD and has since taken some of the most iconic imagery to come out of Afghanistan, as well as working with the Royal Family and appearing on Sky Arts Master of Photography. His company, Schmooly, is a photographic agency that uses military and ex-military photographers and videographers to solve a client's visual problem, whatever it may be. They are as happy working in a corporate setting as they are living out of a rucksack in dangerous and austere environments, wherever in the world clients need them. To date, they've covered events for the Royal Household, car manufacturers, charities, and music concerts among others. Honest, transparent and high quality, Schmooly always delivers on time.

NEIL DAVIES | **FILM MAKER**

A former soldier (Parachute Regiment) with extensive military active service experience. Neil adapted his skills to suit any environment and went on to be an expedition leader, front-line reporter and cameraman – from chasing slave traders on the African continent for Channel Four, to filming erupting volcanos for ITV – before founding dai4films. He is an executive producer with a wealth of TV experience, an award-winning director and producer; Broadcast Documentary of the year for *Raw Spice* (10 million audience on ITV), Artist of the Year for *Nights at the Empire* (Channel Four) and Best Disability Documentary, *Desperate Dan* for BBC. Neil has a 'sixth sense' for great human stories.

ALEX DANDO | **FILM MAKER**

Alex Dando is a third year Media Production student specialising in cinematography. Her aspiration after graduating is to work on feature films as a Director of Photography. Previous shooting experience includes TV and period dramas: *Red Light* and *Wynters Men* (Shoreditch Pictures). Alex has spent time working on multiple projects such as the spoken word poem *Woman* for International Women's Day; *Sonder*, a short film about strangers who help each other find their own peace, and a documentary about female liberation which has been accepted into the INDIS Film Festival. Most recently, she's worked with the company Little Gem TV on a five week internship with their new show *Curvy Girls on the Catwalk*. As well as this, Alex has been wildcard runner for Storyvault films on the show *Landscape Artist of the Year* (Sky Arts). As well as her current work helping marketing for *Soldier On*, Alex is proficient in editing and colour grading using a number of tehcnologies and has also recently worked as an editor on *Professor Hallux's Antibiotics* for kids' TV 'Funkids'.

SEB CANNINGS | **PRODUCTION MANAGER AND DESIGNER**

A graduate of the Central School of Speech and Drama, Seb joined Gary Beestone Events and Theatre as assistant production manager for *Harry Potter and the Cursed Child*. Now supporting all areas of the business, recent production credits as PM include: *Around the World in 80 Days* for Kenny Wax, *Wilde Creatures for Tall Stories, Blueberry Toast* and *The One* for The Soho Theatre and *Dick Whittington and his Cat* for Oxford Playhouse. Seb is trained in IOSH Managing Safely, CIEH Level 2 Award in Fire Safety Principals and Emergency First Aid at Work.

NICK SHATFORD | **COMPANY ADVISOR**

Hailing originally from Leicester, Nick has worked as a mental health professional for over 27years. He is Health and Wellbeing Manager for Stoll and served in an advisory capacity with them for four years and before that, with the CVP since 2011. His role has evolved into a company manager and Nick supports all members of the company on all levels inside the rehearsal sessions and out.

IAIN MCCALLUM | **PRESS**

Previously Head of Press and PR at leading independent television producer, Tiger Aspect Productions, Iain is a Senior Communications and Media specialist with a successful track record in television, film and the arts. His current client base draws from the worlds of television, film, fashion, education, politics and personality. Iain's campaigns are notable for how they break away from the tried, tested and predictable. An abiding passion is giving voice to the under-represented and bringing projects alive by turning conventional PR on its head. Iain delivers memorable, multi-platform, fully-integrated communications campaigns; creating these for some the the UK's best known drama, entetainment, comedy, factual and childrens; and animation series resulting in numerous BAFTA, RTS, Emmy, Ivor Novello, Rose d'Or and Broadcast nominations and awards. He has been a fan of Jonathan Guy Lewis' work for many years and is particularly excited to be working with the cast and crew of *Soldier On*, a production which brings together so many of the things Iain holds dear: entertainment, creativity and important issues deserving of attention and a wider audience.

ANNA ARTHUR | **PRESS**

Anna Arthur PR is a leading independent PR consultancy, specialising in arts, culture and heritage PR. Her clients include Alexandra Palace, Edinburgh Comedy Awards, London International Mime Festival, Creative New Zealand, Shubbak Festival, King's College London, the Holt Festival and OHMI (one handed musical instrument) Trust. Previously, as one half of Arthur Leone, she's worked with a number of West End producers including Nimax Theatres, Raymond Gubbay, Danny Moar, James Seabright Productions, Vakhtangov Theatre Company, Sovremennik Theatre Company, the Royal and Derngate, Bath Theatre Royal, Bill Kenwright Ltd, Menier Chocolate Factory, Oxford Playhouse and the Roundhouse.

KAIJA LARKE | **PRESS**
@kaijaLarke

ROMAN BACA | **MARKETING**

Roman Baca is a classically trained ballet dancer and choreographer. In 2000, recognizing his desire to defend the vulnerable, he took a hiatus from dance and enlisted in the United States Marine Corps, serving as a machine-gunner and fire-team leader in Fallujah, Iraq during the Iraq War. After the war, Baca returned to dance and co-founded Exit12 Dance Company, which tells veterans' stories choreographically, to increase cross-cultural understanding and heal divisions. He has choreographed and championed danceworks exploring the military veteran experience and the impact of war on civilians and families. Baca has presented his work in the United States and United Kingdom. He's also led choreographic workshops at schools, universities and veterans' centres to inspire military veterans, victims of war, and civilians through the power of dance. Baca is currently pursuing an MFA in choreography at the Trinity Laban Conservatoire of Music and Dance, London. His research there is two-fold: to expand his practice and solidify his voice as a choreographer, and to research, choreographically, the psycho-somatic connection in soldiers resulting from the embodiment of military training. Part of his studies involve a choreographed work to Igor Stravinsky's *Le Sacre du Printemps*, collaborating with military veterans, dancers, musicians, and artists. He also researches and volunteers with London-based charitable organizations to connect military veterans to the performing arts.

CLAIRE ACKLING | **ASSISTANT PRODUCER**

Claire spent a large part of her career as a radio producer with the BBC. Specialising in live sport and events. Often producing coverage of Olympics, World Cups and big news sories. Events have remained a focus since leaving the BBC bosom, using her skills to branch out as a press officer, floor manager, media trainer and broadcast manager. She'll give anything a go if it sounds like a laugh! Recent highlights have been: her involvement on a broadcast team for the Royal Wedding, the Referendum and Wimbledon. She's often found out and about in London, supporting new theatre productions – and some old. A news junkie, with a love of film, travel and expensive spas.

FREDDIE LYNCH| **ASSISTANT PRODUCER**

Freddie is an aspiring theatre producer from London. Having recently left university, he is delighted to be working on his first professional show with *Solider On*. At University College London he was the Students' Union Arts Officer and produced 8 shows with UCL Musical Theatre Society. Freddie has produced shows at the Edinburgh Fringe and in the Shaw Theatre and at RADA Studios. He is currently producing the UK premiere of an updated version of Tim Rice's *From Here To Eternity* in the Bloomsbury Theatre. Twitter **@FreddieLynch10**

SAMARA-ALANA SMITH | **ASSISTANT PRODUCER**

Samara graduated from King`s College London with an M.Sc. in War and Psychiatry. She also has a BA (Hons.) in Theatre and Performance from Plymouth University and a National Diploma Level 3 in Professional Musical Theatre from The Urdang Academy. Samara performed as a professional performer before a period of ill-health, and is very grateful to have had the opportunity to transition to the production team, thanks to the Soldiers' Arts Academy. Having written dissertations on both how the arts are used to boost morale in the 21st Century British Military, and how the arts can be used to help with recovery from psychological trauma caused by conflict; and due to her family's military background, Samara feels that the work of the Soldiers' Arts Academy is of the utmost importance. She hopes that *Soldier On* will help to create a sustainable model for the use of the arts with veterans and the military community. Samara has enjoyed working towards performing again, and would like to thank everyone involved with The Soldiers' Arts Academy and this production of *Soldier On* for their support.

CLAIRE WESLEY | **ASSISTANT PRODUCER**

Claire trained as a lawyer before becoming an accountant. She worked as a partner in PwC and Deloitte. She now fills a variety of non-executive and charitable roles largely based in Yorkshire. She is interested in the arts and is Chair of the Arts Society Ebor. She loves singing.

HELENA WESTERMAN | **ASSISTANT PRODUCER**

Helena trained at the London Academy of Music and Dramatic Art and has worked as an actor, writer and producer. She's currently the Co-Artistic Director of Rascal Theatre, which she set up in 2016. Producing credits include: *St George is Cross* (Edinburgh Festival); *An Act of Kindness* (Lion and Unicorn Theatre, Theatre503, Edinburgh Festival, VAULT Festival, Old Joint Stock Theatre) and *The Melting Pot* (Finborough Theatre). Twitter **@helenawesterman @rascaltheatre**

ROSE WETHERBY | **ASSISTANT PRODUCER**

Rose has always loved theatre and has studied both drama, film and photography at school. She has made a few short films and is thrilled to be given the opportunity of working as an assistant to the Producer. Next year, Rose will be heading off to Newcastle University.

MADELEINE KASSON | **PRODUCTION ASSISTANT**
@MadeleineKasson

MARK HOPKINS, WE'LL MIND YOUR OWN BUSINESS | **ACCOUNTING**
www.wmyob.co.uk

BLINKHORNS | **ACCOUNTING**
www.blinkhorns.co.uk

DEWYNTERS | **MARKETING CONSULTANTS**

Leading independent arts, events and live entertainment marketing specialists, their work in theatre, museums, attractions, sport and music is seen right across the globe. **www.dewynters.com**

THE PRODUCERS WOULD LIKE TO THANK
THE FOLLOWING WHO HAVE MADE
THIS PRODUCTION POSSIBLE

Jonathan Lewis would like to thank all serving ex military personnel and their families who have kindly agreed to speak to him and who have helped to raise awareness of the challenges of returning to civilian life. In particular he would like to thank the following:

The casts of all the productions of *Our Boys*

Bravo 22 Company's participants of *Boots at the Door*

The Soldiers' Arts Academy and everyone involved in the development of *Soldier On:*

A special thanks to Max Hamilton-Mackenzie for creating the website
soldiersartsacademy.com

Also thanks to:

Mrs Alex Page
Mrs Rachel Dawkins
Jamie Isbell
R Bradley
Esta Charkham
James Dangerfield
Richard Hornsby
Ray Eves
Simon Fielder
Justine Gilbert
Caroline Kent
Jo Jo Macari
J Hughes-Morgan
Tom Moutchi
Richard Jeremy
J A Simmonds
David Solomon
Philip Long
Kate Pennington
Peter Snipp
Marcia Sommerford
Imogen Stubbs
Jonathan Stapleton
Phoebe Stapleton
H Thompson

Corinne Zak
Melanie and Alan Craig
Liz Barber
Elizabeth Healey
Simon de Cintra
Jon G'eden
Jo Bishop
Hadley Smith
Philippa Chapman
Jess Pryce-Jones
Martin Hamilton
Kate Miles
Jan Evans
Robbie Morgan
Hugh Wooldridge
Nicola Pollard
Andy and Sophie Nyman
Claire Goose
Sean Gilder
Lloyd Owen
Jo Dow
Jan Ravens
David Trevaskis

Julia Lindsay
Julia Goodman
Mike Cornwall
Francesca Simon
Martin Stamp
Andrew Tsai
Chloe Harbour
Chelsea FC
Michele Wyckoff Smith
Maurilia Simpson
KT Parker
Marcia Brown
Rahel Eyob
Anthony and Georgina Andrews
Jessica Howe
Charlotte Sawers
Azzi Glasser
Thomas Craig

Working in partnership with the Royal Foundation and supported by the local Public Services Team at EY and by The Armed Forces Covenant Fund Trust

**ARMED FORCES
COVENANT**

THANKS ALSO TO

The following charities and companies for their kind support:

Old Possums Practical Trust

Forman's Fish Island Restaurant

Golden Bottle Trust

Wander Curtis Wines

Rehearsal space at
Holy Innocents Church Hammersmith

Red Sky July

Stoll

WWTW

Shakespeare's Globe

Serco

BFBS

Oliver Wyman

James Anda

RG Media

Faber and Faber

Suited and Booted

Maurice Sparrow Photography

Interrupt the Routine

Deerness Distillery

Special thanks to the following:

Lord Lloyd Webber and everyone at The Other Palace theatre,
Brigadier Fred Hargreaves OBE, Dr. Paula Holt, The Lord Dannatt,
Graham Bird, Lt. Col. Joanne Young, Jamie Campbell,
Union Jack Club, Stuart and Adelle Brown, Rob Blackwood.
Les Gordon, Ellie Nunn, Toby Faber,Doug Faulkner, Charles Dean,
Dr Maria Lenn, Angus Murray, Dave, Cheryl and George Taylor,
Simon and Anna Trussler, Elaine Caulfield, Pamela Deakin,
Adam Wander, Lance Forman, Ian Grant, Claire Bishop,
Richard Hatch BFBS, Lt. Col. (Retd.) Stewart Hill, Karen Hodgson,
Heather Saunders, The Woodville – Gravesend,
The Playground Theatre – London, The North Wall – Oxford,
Exeter Northcott Theatre and York Theatre Royal.

SOLDIER ON

JONATHAN LEWIS

Soldier On

THE SOLDIERS' ARTS ACADEMY PRESS

First published in February 2018
by Soldiers' Arts Academy Press
2 Laurier Road, London NW5 1SG

New edition published in October 2018

Designed and typeset by Country Setting,
Kingsdown, Kent CT14 8ES

Printed in England by Biddles
King's Lynn, Norfolk PE32 1SF

A CIP record for this book is available from the British Library

ISBN 978-1-9998488-3-5

Characters

Rickshaw

Maggie

Beth
also plays Chrissy

Trees

Woody

Flaps

Sal
also plays Paula

Sophie

Tanya
also plays Sonya

James / Jenny
also plays Cameron
and Voice of Darren

Harry

Len

Jacko
also plays Donny

Tom

TC

Hoarse

Part One

In the darkness, we hear a long low sustained note played on a double bass. After a few beats it is joined by the voice of a man, Rickshaw. Lights slowly fade up on him.

Rickshaw (*voice-over*) Once upon a time there lived a young dragon called Ryan. And all the other young dragons would fly about and breathe fire, but not Ryan. He grew up to be the biggest and strongest of them, but still he wouldn't breathe fire. Until one day the king decreed the strongest and bravest of all the dragons must fly away across the sea to fight the evildoers threatening his kingdom, and young Ryan was compelled to go.

> *Rickshaw walks slowly down to the front of the stage. He wears a green boiler suit, black T-shirt, and army boots.*
> *The rest of the cast appear, all wearing the same. They walk forward and join Rickshaw. The whole cast is assembled.*
> *They all come to attention. This becomes a dance (think Michael Flatley, Riverdance, Stomp and a clog dance but in army boots). They get more energised through the drumming. Then suddenly it stops. They are all at attention. In silence, and in their assembled ranks, they all take off both boots and place them as pairs on the floor. This happens in a ritualised slow motion at the same time. They exit, leaving Rickshaw at the centre, on his own. Some deliberately bash into him, provoking him.*

(*To the audience, but holding his ear as if on the phone*) And when Ryan returned home, he'd learned to breathe

7

the fiercest of fire. But now every time he tried to help, the people would say 'Ryan! You're a danger. Go away. Your fire will be the death of us all.'

Rickshaw raises a fist to one of them. It is Jacko, who tentatively puts a friendly hand over Rickshaw's fist and lowers it. The last one to go is James, who looks at Rickshaw with a mixture of sadness and despair.

So, Ryan went to live alone in a cave outside the castle walls, then he wouldn't hurt any more of the King's subjects.

He is interrupted by small arms fire from a distance. This continues and gets louder underneath the rest of this speech.

And Ryan learned to live out his life in the shade and shadows, rather than the sun and be free. And that's where . . . That's . . . . right, I've got to go now kids. Lily, Barney. I'll record some more laters, alright? Daddy loves you. Big kiss, Princess. Big kiss all.

A loud explosion resonates around the space.
   Blackout. Rickshaw disappears off stage. The explosion cross-fades into the news – details of another fatal incident involving the military in Afghan.
   On the back wall appears:

ONE
A YEAR AGO: THE RECCE

We hear the sound of someone hoovering just off.
   Lights up on: a stage hand (Hoarse), who comes on and sweeps the boots from the stage.
   Maggie comes out onto the stage. She is now dressed in jeans and a blouse. She smiles nervously as she walks to the centre.

Maggie (*tentative, to the unseen director in the audience*) Hiya. Am I in the right place? (*Holds up a flyer, expecting an answer, but there is none.*) The auditions for the play. I haven't prepared anything. But I could sing something. I am in the choir.

Beth strides forward. She wears jeans and leather jacket.

Beth (*Welsh, to the unseen director in the audience*) Alright? (*To Elaine.*) Alright, Mags.

Maggie I'm Maggie by the way. This is Beth.

Beth Hiya. So, what's the crack? Just to say, I can't stay much beyond half past as I've got to get back for the kittens.

Maggie (*smiling*) Ah, has she had the kittens?

Beth Yeah, gorgeous, but His Highness is on deployment, so no help on that front.

Maggie Her Gavin's in The Rifles. My Cameron's Artillery.

Beth First deployment.

Maggie He's only twenty.

Beth (*pointing to Elaine*) Proud mum alert. (*Mouthing to the director and making a gesture that Cameron's 'hot'.*) He's very fit.

Maggie (*shutting Beth up*) Thank you, Bethany.

Beth Did she tell you we're in the choir?

Maggie Not the original.

Beth But we *are*:

Maggie *and* **Beth** 'Aldershot's Singing Sensation.'

During this, Teressa (Trees) has been hovering upstage.

She holds a violin case in one hand and a piece of paper, a flyer, in the other.

Maggie Hiya.

Beth Don't be shy, love.

Trees Is this the auditions for the play?

Beth That's what it says on the doors.

Trees I'm not sure I'm eligible. I'm not Military.

Beth (*holding a flyer up*) So which part of 'Military Community' on the flyer wasn't clear then, love?

Trees My dad was Naval Reserve.

Maggie (*seeking affirmation from the director*) Well, that counts, doesn't it?

Trees He was in the Falklands. HMS *Sheffield*.

Maggie (*grimacing*) The one that went down?

Beth (*relieved*) Well, that's alright then.

Warren (Woody) Woods barges on, striding to the centre of the stage. He wears a summer pork-pie hat and shorts.

Woody Stand back, folks, the talent has arrived. I'm here on serious business. (*Taking up the pose of a Shakespearian actor at the Globe.*) 'To be or not . . . ' (*Looking around at the motley crew, underwhelmed.*) Fuck me. It's not exactly *X Factor* is it?!

Flaps enters, looking for Woody. He has a crash helmet in one hand and wears a biker's jacket emblazoned with several patches including ISIS Hunting Permit and a poppy patch.

Flaps Oi, Woody. What you doing?

Woody I'm thesping, mate.

Flaps Thesping?

Woody Acting with one leg. AWOL! I wouldn't be able to learn actual lines though cos of the drugs. But I could do what Jonny Depp does. He has an earpiece cos he can't learn lines.

Beth Johnny Depp?

Maggie Rubbish.

Beth *The* Jonny Depp?!

Woody It's all them drugs. We've got a lot in common, me and Jonny.

Flaps (*getting more impatient*) Oi, Woody!

Beth You're talking out of your arse, you are.

Maggie It's Woody, is it?

Woody Yes, ma'am. And this is my assistant, who will also be auditioning for the part of my manservant assistant.

Flaps Will you fuck off!

Woody Can you take pity on him? He's not always this ugly. Bit of make-up always works wonders.

They all look at Flaps, who shakes his head and goes.

Woody Where are you going? (*To the women.*) Temperamental or what?! (*Winking at the women.*) Rev up the engine, ladies, but don't start without us.

He follows Flaps off.

Beth Charming.

Rickshaw enters.

Rickshaw Excuse me.

Beth Not another one.

Rickshaw Did Woody really come in here and do some Shakespeare?

Trees It wasn't Shakespeare.

Rickshaw (*to the director in the audience*) It's my fault. I sort of dared him.

Beth Excuse me, there is a queue actually, if you want to audition. Cos I haven't got long, see.

Rickshaw No, no, no, you're alright, love. (*Laughs to himself and shakes his head.*) What's it for, anyway?

Trees gives him her flyer.

Maggie A play about the Military.

Rickshaw What?

Beth (*spelling it out for a dummy*) Military community.

Rickshaw Well, that'll have them queuing around the block.

Woody comes back on, followed by Flaps.

Woody Hey! I forgot to say – I sing as well. Anything you want. You name it I'll sing it. (*It suddenly becomes a rap.*) You itch and I'll scratch it. Double tempo double time. I'll make it fit and I'll give you the rhyme. Hold my crutch and I'll grime. Dig it out from the rock and roll, out of a hole, to bear you my soul, death toll, then you make up your mind, when you see what you find, if I be panning for gold or just recycl'ng the old, cos I'm unwrapping the wrap and I'll take me the bow. (*He spins around and does a bow.*) In the here and the now.

Rickshaw You really going to do this?

Flaps Course he's not going to do this. (*Grabs the flyer from Rickshaw and gives it back to Trees.*)

Woody Why not? Show my sensitive side.

Flaps You haven't got a sensitive side. You're about as sensitive as a fucking IED!

Woody And you're about as funny as an anal prolapse! (*Going.*) And an IED is sensitive. you stupid fuckwit.

The women leave as well, leaving Rickshaw on his own.

Rickshaw Here's one for you. Sergeant Major says to me: I didn't see you in camouflage training this morning son. Thank you very much, sir (*Grins, salutes and goes.*)

Loud music begins. Intro to Taylor Swift, 'Shake It Off', karaoke version.
Sophie comes on, and starts singing and dancing. Sal won't come on the stage with her.

Sophie
  I stay up too late
  Got nothing in my brain
  That's what people say
  That's what people say
  I go on too many dates
  But I can't make them stay
  At least that's what people say
  That's what people say.

Sal takes over singing.

Sal
  But I keep cruising
  Can't stop, won't stop moving
  It's like I got this music
  In my mind

Sal *and* **Sophie**

Saying it's gonna be alright
'Cause the players gonna play, play, play
And the haters gonna hate, hate, hate
Baby I'm just gonna shake, shake, shake
Shake it off, shake it off
Heartbreakers gonna break, break, break
And the fakers gonna fake, fake, fake,
I'm just gonna shake, shake, shake
Shake it off, shake it off
I never miss.

The music is cut off. The girls are a bit breathless.

Harry (*from the back of the auditorium*) Thank you.
Next.

Sophie and Sal still talk through their mics

Sophie What? No, wait. Obviously, that's something
we've just thrown together.

Sal Thrown together, yup.

Sophie I'm Sophie. My Donny's a corporal with Three
Para. He's done one two Afghan tours. One Iraq. He was
blown up in Helmand last time. Didn't lose anything
though, thank God. Well, I know he's got bits missing
and that –

Sal Like his marbles.

Sophie Yeah, but he didn't lose anything important, like
limbs or anything.

Sal And I'm Sal. I'm a doctor and volunteer reservist.
So's my partner.

Sophie She's a doctor.

Sal Yup. She's a doctor. We're both doctors.

Sophie Sal kept a Para alive when they got pinned down under fire! Made them sing 'It's Raining Men' to keep him conscious. And you've heard what her singing's like.

Sal Oi!

They notice James hovering at the back of the stage.

James (*nervous, but 'up'*) Hello. I'm er . . . sorry. My name's, um . . . Actually, I'm not sure if this is er . . . this, er . . . Sorry. I'll just, er . . . Excuse me.

He hurries off.

Blackout.

Lights up as Harry (the Director) comes on through the audience, holding a big 'director's' file. He is joined by Len on the stage. Len is wearing a blazer and regimental tie.

Harry Len?

Len Yes?

Harry Why are we so short of men? I was told the guys would be up for this.

Len Not by me you weren't, pal. They all think it's . . .

Harry What? Too touchy-feely? Pin them down, Len. Don't take no for an answer.

Len You don't want to scare them off.

Harry It's not the Somme, Len. It's a play.

Len We *are* trying, Harry, but we haven't done anything like this before.

Harry Well, we've got to do something different.

Len I told you, get some sport in the play. The lads are a lot less threatened by sport. And there's always Prince Harry and Meghan. Do a play about the Invictus Games?

Harry NO! It can't be about the Invictus bloody Games.

Len Well, you're in charge. I'm just here to facilitate that's all.

Harry (*changing the subject*) I liked Woody though.

Len No . . . too disruptive.

Harry Good. Shake 'em up. And the other lads with him. Do you think we could get them back?

Len That's the thing, Harry. They're not very reliable. That's why I don't think this thing is going –

Len *and* **Harry** – to work.

Harry Yes, thank you, Len. You've made your views crystal clear.

Len Forewarned is forearmed, Harry. (*Thinks.*) Couldn't some of the women pretend to be men?

Harry Pretend?

Len To be men. Yes.

Harry What? 'Man up'?

Len (*enthusing about the idea*) Exactly. Some of the women *were* very masculine, Harry.

Harry Yeah, that's not really going to work.

Len You're not going to fix them by doing a play. (*Pointing to the wings.*) They can't act. Not this rag-tag lot.

Harry It's about daring greatly, Len. Being in the arena.

Len just looks at Harry. He won't back down.

Harry Just bring me more men. (*Knowing he is going to make the joke with Len's name rhyming with men.*) Len.

Len And what do you get out of this?

Harry God. you're good. Len. You've rumbled me. I'm a mole trying to undermine the military by turning all the veterans into poncy, spineless actors. I just want to do a play. Len. Real stories, real soldiers, veterans.

Len You're wasting your time, pal. And mine. And all our money. Look, if you train to do this job, you should expect violence. That's what you sign up for. What kind of impression does this give? Soft. You can't make soldiers by being soft.

Harry They're not soldiers any more, Len.

Lights snap up on Colonel Tom Gordon (late forties). He stands with a stick.

Tom (*mid-conversation*) And then Bastion grew to the size, they say, of Reading.

Harry And a lot less dangerous.

Tom What?

Harry Than Reading on a Saturday night. Bastion grew to – (*There's tumbleweed.*) No never mind.

Tom I take it, it's not going to be a comedy then this play.

Rickshaw and Flaps drift on at the sides and listen.

Rickshaw It was only when you got out of Bastion that the trouble really started. At the FOBs.

Harry FOBs?

Tom (*clarifying*) Forward Operating Bases. Fanning out. Spider's web.

Flaps Usually company strength.

Rickshaw Not up near Kijaki. Only troop-strength up there. Thirty-four days straight we came under fire.

Harry (*horrified*) Thirty four?!

Rickshaw On the day I was dropped at Kijaki, with my best mate Big Dave, an RPG landed about ten feet away. We was blown right across the roof. That's when I did my hearing in this ear.

He points out a hearing aid in his left ear.

Flaps Pardon?

Rickshaw That's when I did the hearing in this – oh, fuck off.

Harry (*turning back to Tom*) Look, I'm still trying to get my head around the fact you had a stroke while you were on your last tour of Helmand.

Tom Mini-stroke. Yeah. But compared to what was happening to some of the other guys, I didn't want to make a fuss. So, I kept it under my belt.

Harry Was it brought on by the heat?

Tom Yup. Possibly, although it was more likely linked to the prostate and bowel cancer. But the good news is the green tea and ginger worked wonders for the droopy jaw. So apart from that, I'm tip-top and raring to go.

Harry My God.

Tom But the good news is the green tea and ginger worked wonders for the droopy jaw.

Beat. He doesn't know what to say – looks at his piece of paper.

Harry It's Tom?

Tom Yes.

Harry Colonel Tom Gordon.

Tom Yup.

Harry Scots Guards.

Flaps Eh up, the Jocks!

Tom (*not amused*) First Battalion, yup. But I don't . . . er . . . The rank. Not any more.

Harry Well, I'm Harry.

Tom And you're OC?

Harry What?

Tom Well, aren't you?

Harry Obsessive-compulsive?

Tom I beg your pardon?

Flaps He's asking are you in charge, sir.

Tom Officer Commanding.

Harry (*suddenly getting it*) Oh I see. (O-I-C).

Flaps O-I-C?

Rickshaw Now I'm really fucking confused.

Tom Look. I'm not sure how effective I'd be with all this. But I'd like to give it a go, if you'll have me. I want to do it for my children. And for my wife Caroline. Get me out from under her feet. Oh, and just to say getting to the loo can be a bit of an issue.

Harry You and me both.

Jacko walks forward.

Jacko (*stutters*) I'm Jacko Nicholson. 3 Ppppp-Para. Left 2011. Best years of my life. But hasn't been too great since leaving. Had a bit of trouble. But I'm trying to get back on my feet now. Drugs and that. Gambling. But-but-but I've put that all behind me now.

Harry You sure? Cos we can't have any –

Jacko (*reassuring*) Absolutely positive sir. Learnt my lesson. Now I only back certainties.

Harry's face falls.

That was a joke. I was going to say only bbback certainties which is why I'm here.

TC walks forward.

TC Terrence Cornelius, sir. RAF. Sergeant Engineer. Chinooks.

Harry Thanks for coming down, Terrence.

TC I came out in 2010.

Harry Did you? You came out in 2010.

TC Roger that.

Harry That was brave of you. Not easy to be gay in the forces.

TC I beg your pardon?

Harry To come out.

TC Of the RAF.

Harry Of the RAF. (*Cringing at his misunderstanding.*)

TC I was in a crash. Chinook went down.

Harry Blimey.

TC I'm hoping to get involved. Sound or something like that.

Harry And acting?

TC (*laughing to himself*) You got to be joking. I'm up at Mike Jackson's.

Jacko You Mike Jackson's as well? I knew I'd seen you there.

TC It's nice up there. They look after you, you know?

Tom Sheltered accommodation, Harry. For Veterans.

Jacko Bit bbbbasic but you get your own room and that.

TC And there's counselling.

Jacko Ppppp. TSD. I never used to stutter before. Fuckin' does my head in. Sorry. 'Scuse my French.

Hoarse is on stage with Len.

Hoarse (*mid-anecdote, pointing to Len, enjoying telling it*) So he says, 'I'm that hungry I could eat the arse out of a dead leper.'

Len *Chew.*

Hoarse What?

Len 'Chew the arse out of a dead lepper.'

Hoarse So he says 'I'm that hungry I could eat the arse out of a dead –

Len (*interrupting – he's frustrated Hoarse is screwing up the joke*) That's enough. Hoarse was a full screw when I were his Company Sergeant Major.

Harry A what?

Len Corporal. In my Company. Yorkshire Regiment. (*To Hoarse.*) You got your second stripe up? Just. Very good lad is Hoarse. When he's not trying to tell anecdotes.

Hoarse (*continuing the anecdote*) So he says 'I'm that hungry I could chew the arse off of a –'

Harry (*interrupting – to put everyone out of their misery*) Yes, thank you, Hoarse.

Len I think the moment's passed, Hoarse. (*To Harry.*) The horse has bolted, Harry!

Harry And have you acted before?

Hoarse No. I've been volunteered. (*Looks at Len.*)

Len (*to Harry*) Good luck.

Blackout.

TWO

CONTACT

The whole cast assembles. We hear 'It's Raining Men'.

Len Alright. (*To the whole group.*) Listen in. I'm Len. And we are producing this –

He is interrupted by Flaps.

Flaps (*excited – sings and plays the air guitar, then drums*) 'Play'.

Len Rehabilitation event. (*Pointing to a signing-in sheet on the table to the side.*) There's a signing in sheet out there. Consent forms in blue, feedback forms in green, health and safety in pink, for the ladies. And Tanya, where's Tanya, has very kindly made us a fabulous cake for our tea break. So, a big thank you to Tanya.

Beth does a wolf whistle. Others clap and make positive gestures towards Tanya.

Tanya It's nothing. It's just a gin-and-tonic loaf cake, laced with organic lemon zest and fizzy slimline tonic syrup topping.

Len (*getting their attention back and reading*) 'Company Soldier On' will be meeting here weekly, nineteen hundred hours to twenty-two thirty leading up to D Day, when you will be attempting the delivery three times in total.

Harry 'Performances'. Len.

Len Performances. And just to clarify, this will be expenses only, is that clear?

Jacko (*this is news to Jacko, who stands, pissed off*) Oh. What!

Len Sit down, Nicholson. Apparently – (*Reading.*) 'The reward will be in the doing, because it's going to be an antidote to man's inhumanity to man. And not to mention it's going to be fun as well.' Any questions? No. In that case I'm going to officially introduce you all to Harry.

Harry Thank you, Len. Let's go around, say who we are. Say one fact about ourselves that might be true . . . and one that might not be true.

Len What?

Harry A fact or a lie.

James Why?

Harry Why not? Might be fun. A hook?

James A hook.

Harry A hook. Yup.

James (*not convinced*) Right. A hook.

Harry Jacko? Start us off.

Jacko Okay. I'm Jacko. I *am* an alcoholic. So, I can't have any of that gin and tonic ccccake, which I'm gutted about. And I had a serious gambling addiction, and . . . (*Sheepish.*) I, er, kkkkilled people in Afghanistan.

Rickshaw Well, that's lowered the tone. Where do we go from there then?

Sal (*interrupting*) It's not a competition.

Harry (*trying to move the conversation on*) Guys, please.

He gestures towards Sophie.

Sophie Hello, I'm Sophie. Mother of three. My partner Donny has PTSD, and we live in the shadow of that. He has good days and bad days, as do we all. But I suppose it means he's not always able to be the dad that he'd like to be . . . or the partner. We're waiting for him to be medically discharged.

Sal indicates that Soph should wrap it up.

And . . . I can fit six Ferrero Rocher in my mouth. Oh, and a Mini Twix.

Harry Right. Flip?

Flaps Flaps. My friends and that, they all call me Flaps.

Rickshaw You haven't got any friends.

Flaps Oi! I'm a tankie. Divorced. One boy. And I hate motorbikes.

Rickshaw smiles and holds up Flaps' crash helmet.

Maggie I'm Maggie. Divorced. Twice. I'm fed up with moving. Done it nineteen times in twenty-two years. My son Cameron is twenty and on his first deployment.

Beth That was actually well more than one fact, Mags.

Maggie Was it? Sorry. I'm not very good at lying.

Beth Or counting.

Maggie Haven't got the face for it. Everything's written right there. (*Gestures to her face.*)

Sophie Windows of the soul.

Maggie Sorry?

They all look at her.

Sophie The eyes, I mean. That's what they say?

Jacko Do they?

Sophie Don't they? Maybe not.

Harry gestures to Tom.

Tom Hello, I'm Tom. I've had a stroke, and cancer, which is why this thing – (*Meaning his own body.*) doesn't seem to work as well as it should. And, er . . . I once shoplifted a Mars bar.

Hoarse Oh no! Shock horror! We've all done that, sir.

Maggie Speak for yourself.

Tom And please don't call me sir.

Hoarse Sorry, sir. (*Catching himself.*) Sorry.

Tom Tom.

Hoarse Tom.

Beth I'm Beth. Bethany. I'm happily married.

Maggie laughs.

And . . . er . . . Thinking about that one . . . I'm happily married to Gavin . . . who's a Hobbit.

Flaps Charming.

Maggie She means he's small and not very friendly,

Tanya Oh, like Jeremy Kyle.

Beth Er, yeah, like Jeremy Kyle.

Trees Hello. I'm Teressa. But everyone calls me Trees. I'm from Portsmouth. It's actually Havant. But no one's heard of Havant.

Flaps No, you're right. I haven't.

Trees Is he for real? Are you for real? (*Beat.*) And I'm, like, slightly Asperger's.

Rickshaw I'm Rickshaw. Cos one time when we was on leave in Cyprus, I hired a pedalo, and gave all the lads a ride, so they gave me the nickname Rickshaw. How lame is that? And I like Asparagus as well.

Len Asperger's not asparagus, you numty!

Rickshaw What?

Flaps (*clarifying for Rickshaw*) She said Asperger's, not fucking asparagus.

Len Oi! Language. Ladies present.

Sal Where? Right. I'm Sal. I've got Post-Traumatic Stress Disorder. I've raised nearly seventy thousand pounds from the marathons I've run.

Flaps (*amazed*) What? In cash?!

Trees No. In Mars bars.

Beth That's amazing.

Sal I think everyone should run at least one marathon in their life.

Hoarse I'm running one every day, love.

Sal Really? You look like you've been eating one.

Tanya Hello, everybody. I'm Tanya I married my husband Baz after we met in Iraq on Telic V. You see Baz was SF and –

Harry Sorry, Tanya. SF?

Jacko Schizophrenic.

Tanya Special Forces.

Jacko Same thing.

Tanya Baz fought in the first Gulf War. Six months after he came back on Arctic training, he got lost from his section . . . They found him, but he'd died. I was an armourer. (*onders whether she should share this.*) And I miss him.

James Hello, everybody I'm James. I was a Flight Lieutenant in the RAF Regiment. I know this is going to sound a bit, um . . . weird, but I know all the words to the film *Pretty Woman*. I've seen it, well, my current count is thirty-four times.

Tom Why on earth would you want to see Pretty Woman thirty-four times?

James I just . . . I don't know . . . It was . . . she was what I wanted to be when I was younger.

Tom What? A prostitute?!

James No.

Rickshaw It's about a hooker.

James (*overriding him*) I wanted to be a woman.

Jacko You what?

Beth Amazing.

Len (*quietly*) Oh dear.

James I'm in the process of gender realignment.

Jacko (*confiding to James*) You'll probably find Len's got a form for that.

James The main thing to understand is that gender isn't binary.

Maggie (*leaning over to ask Beth*) Isn't what?

James Binary.

Maggie Right. Okay. Isn't it?

Sophie Sorry, it does actually raise the question of what you'd like us to call you.

James (*thinks*) I'm okay with James or Jamie for now, but when I actually start transitioning, which will happen before I have my surgeries, I would like you to start calling me 'they'.

Len (*thinking he misheard*) Beg your pardon?

James They.

Len Who?

James They. T–H–E–Y.

Len Right. They.

James I'm not ready to take a binary option yet, so I've been advised to try the singular plural.

Len Singular plural.

Jacko You alright, Len? Or do you need a bit of a lie-down?

James I'm hoping the process won't get in the way of the play.

Harry No. No, you . . . you do what you have to, and we'll work around you. They. The change. It's very brave of you to want to do this, James. And to share it with us.

James You said it was going to be a safe place to be myself. And I've got nothing else to lose. Believe me when you hit rock bottom, like I know a lot of you here have, the only way is up. I've been so dishonest about myself for so long.

Harry TC?

Sophie What does TC stands for exactly?

TC Terrence Cornelius. That's why I stick to TC. My fact of information is I have a son, who is twenty-four.

Sophie Top Cat junior?

TC (*smiling*) Darren. He joined up in 2012. But sadly he lost his right leg and right hand in an IED in Helmand Province. November 24th 2014.

There is an empathetic response from the rest of the group towards TC.

TC I don't get to see him as much as I'd like. Being here. He and Sonya, his mother, live in London now. We're separated. Til I sort myself out. It was a bit of a shock . . . what happened to Darren, and I didn't, um . . . deal with it, you know, as well as I could.

Harry Hoarse?

Rickshaw Why do they call you Hoarse, Hoarse?

Beth Well, that's obvious isn't it. He must be hung like / a

Len Oi, Beth! D'you mind?

Hoarse It's not that kind of horse. It's when I'm tanked up . . . I can be a bit voluable. Sound wise.

Jacko (*is that even a word?!*) Voluable!? That's not even a word.

Hoarse Till my voice goes hoarse. Then I've been told I sound like a dying pig.

Sophie That's really horrible, Hoarse. Who told you that?

Len (*after a pause*) No . . . I never said dying.

Harry Len?

Len What?

Harry Fact or a fib.

Len (*shaking his head*) No.

Harry Come on.

Len I'm from Yorkshire, Harry. I don't do fact or fib.

Maggie Oh go on Len. Fact or fib.

They all start chanting 'Fact or fib'.

Len Alright. Alright. Settle down. I am an apiarist.

Rickshaw He's what? He's a fucking rapist?!

They all say to Rickshaw 'Apiarist'.

Len I keep bees. Have done for a couple of years. Ever since . . .

Sophie Since?

Len (*not sure what to say*) It doesn't matter.

Sal What about you, Harry?

Harry Me? Well. (*Thinks for a moment.*) That's a long story for another day. Right now, let's get up and do something.

He tries to get them up but no one moves.

James Hold on, that's a bit unfair. You're not going to share something back?

Sophie Yeah. That's a bit rubbish, Harry.

Harry Okay . . . Well . . . A hundred years ago I used to be in a TV series called *Soldier, Soldier*.

There is a general reaction of surprise.

Maggie I knew I recognised you.

Sal *You* were in *Soldier, Soldier*?

Trees Really?

Harry Yes.

Tanya You?

Harry (*not sure what to say*) Yes. Why not me?

Tanya Go on, Harry. Were you really?

Harry Yes. Actually.

Maggie I used to love *Soldier, Soldier*.

James Who did you play?

Harry I played the Adjutant Tom Forrest. Series six.

Jacko Was it a ggggood part?

Harry Oh, you know.

Jacko No, I don't know. That's why I'm asking.

Tanya Did you have actual lines?

Harry Course I had lines.

Trees Found him.

Sal Where?

Sophie There.

Beth Oh yeah. There he is. Oh dear.

Maggie Age has not been very kind has it, Harry.

Harry What do you mean?

Beth You had a bit more hair then, didn't you?

Rickshaw Fuck me! How old were you there then? Twelve?!

Harry (*getting up*) So, yes that's me. And now let's get up and play something.

He throws the ball in the air again, but no one gets up.

James Why?

Sophie Play what exactly?

Harry Why don't we just see where getting up takes us?

Trees (*gesturing from her seat to the empty space*) Well, at a guess, it's going to take us from over here to over there.

Beth Oh God. It's not going to be like that is it?

Harry Like what?

Beth All knit-your-own-yoghurt and that.

Maggie So where's the script for this play then, Harry?

Harry Ah. Now, we'll be making the script . . . our story, together.

Beth God help us.

Sophie Who's going to be interested in anything we've got to say?

Harry I believe it was Michelangelo who said he wasn't actually sculpting, he was chipping away to reveal the piece of work that was already there.

Jacko That's a Ninja turtle for you.

Harry Your homework is to start writing the story.

Sophie Homework?

Sal Wait?! Whaaat?

Tanya I can't write a story.

Sophie Where am I going to find a story?

Beth I haven't got time.

Sal I'm on nights at the moment, Harry.

Harry It doesn't have to be a tome.

Rickshaw A what?

Harry A tome.

Flaps What's a tome when it's at home?

James It's 'Tome Alone'.

Rickshaw And then you nick all these stories?

Harry No, we weave them –

Rickshaw We weave what?

TC I'm not doing any weaving.

Beth What planet do you think we're from?

Harry Can we park the weaving analogy for a moment?

Tanya I don't mind weaving.

Harry We won't literally be weaving, okay.

Beth This is turning into a bloody waste of time. I have to sort childcare. You should have made this much clearer.

Len Ah, Beth, we will have the crèche up and running for next time –

Beth (*to Len*) Bollocks. There isn't going to be a next time. (*To Harry.*) When we are at choir, we sing. Okay. We rehearse. This isn't doing a play. This is having a wank, if you'll excuse my French.

  Beth goes.

Flaps (*shouting after Beth, amused*) No, Beth. Come off the fence. Say what you really think.

Beth (*from offstage*) Oh shove it up your arse, Flappy!

Len Beth? (*Going out after Beth.*) Oi, Taffy, come back.

  They all now start to get up and disperse.

Harry Look, wait. (*Stopping them.*)) If this isn't for you then go. Now.

  They decide to go. Harry stops them again.

Wait. Wait. We could make something extraordinary. Healing, potentially.

He looks around the team. No one goes.

Tom Alright, Harry. But a plea from a simple man, and a plea I feel on behalf of simple, military left-brain folk. Let's not disappear up our proverbials please.

Harry I'll do my best, Tom.

Tom Thank you.

Harry (*hitting the ball up into the air with his palm*) One.

Flaps gets what Harry is playing and hits the ball into the air next. They all say 'One'. Just before they get to 'Twenty', Woody comes on and catches the ball. There is a negative reaction from the assembled company.

TC (*furious*) Wank buggering fuck cock!

Woody (*looking at everyone looking at him*) Wooah.

Rickshaw Why couldn't you just come in and wait?

Jacko We was playing a gggame.

Hoarse You fucked it for us.

Rickshaw We was just about to get to twenty.

Hoarse You jack bastard, you fucked it for us.

Woody I had a fuckin' thing, alright.

Len (*coming back in with real rage*) Will you stop using that disgusting language and sit down. And give me the ball. Right, I'm closing this thing down. If you can't do a simple thing like that. Right. As you were, Harry.

Harry Thank you, Len. Woody! Fantastic you're here.

Jacko Why does he gggget special treatment?

Harry I think Woody had a few issues finding us.

Woody Yeah, I had a few issues to – (*Mocking Jacko.*) ccccontend with.

Harry And in the spirit of collaboration, Woody, it would be appreciated if we all made our best efforts to get to the rehearsal for the specified time.

Flaps I.e., for the hard of learning, don't be late.

There is a sudden PTSD-fuelled flare up between Woody and Flaps.

Woody Fuck you.

Len Language!

Flaps No, no, no, mate. It's courtesy. Don't try and make it about you.

Woody I'm not trying to make it about me.

Flaps Don't try and blame PTSD. We've all got Post Traumatic Stress.

Maggie Oi!! (*Beat.*) Thank you. Now, apparently, it's going to be very healing throwing this ball in the air.

Sal We're 'getting to know each other'.

Sophie We're playing 'uppsy ballsy'.

Rickshaw Uppsy what?

Sophie Uppsy ballsy.

Rickshaw And this better not be going on YouTube.

Sophie It *is* uppsy ballsy isn't it? Although it's a bit more ballsy uppsy at the moment.

Sal takes the ball off Woody and throws it up into the air. They all start counting the numbers. Blackout. Music.

Moonlight. Trees enters carrying Flaps on her back. They are both drunk and laughing. They are outside and on top of a hill in the Downs.

Trees Right. That's it. You've had your lot. Off!

Flaps Come on, bit further.

Trees You're a lump. And you owe me a drink?

Flaps You said Bonfire's Point.

Trees It *is* Bonfire's Point. Quadruple rum and Red Bull please.

Flaps (*getting up*) That's romantic.

Trees That was the bet. (*Looking out to the imagined Downs and breathing in the night air.*) I love it up here.

Flaps (*takes in the view as well.*) Bit bleak, init?

Trees It's romantic.

Flaps No it's not, it's just . . . bleak.

Trees Smell the air. You can taste it. (*Taking off her shoes.*) Full moon. (*Breathing in again and closing her eyes.*)

Flaps (*looking up at the moon*) You should'a seen the moons we had in Afghan—

Trees screams a long scream.

Oi! Shut up! Oi! What are you doing?

Trees stops screaming but has a fizz about her as a result of screaming.

Flaps What did you do that for?

Trees Go on. I dare you.

Flaps No!

Trees Come on.

Flaps No.

Trees Please.

Flaps Why?

Trees Cos you just feel better when you've done it.

Flaps (*thinks about doing it*) No, it's stupid. It's dangerous.

Trees Just open your mouth, take a breath and the wind will take you. You'll be buzzing. (*Screams again.*)

Flaps (*grabs hold of her and puts his hand over her mouth*) Oi! Stop it! You'll get me arrested.

Trees It's traditional. On a full moon. Werewolves, hormonal women and penguins. (*She howls like a warewolf.*)

> *Flaps tries to stop her howling but she bites his hand. He pulls away from her, checking his hand.*

Flaps You bit me, you nut job!

Trees I'll buy you a drink if you do it.

Flaps You can buy me a frigging plaster and take me to Casualty. I'll need a jab for rabies. I thought we were doing research. Which bit of this is research?

> *Trees turns away from him, closes her eyes and breathes into the wind. Flaps looks at her, then at his hand and then out at the Downs. He lets out a long scream.*

37

Flaps (*surprised with himself*) Bloody hell!

Trees Told you.

They both look out and breathe in the salty air.

Trees Do you reckon Beth's partner really is a Hobbit?

Flaps (*imitating a Hobbit*) 'Oh no Frodooooooo.'

As a Hobbit/monkey, Flaps tries to tickle Trees. They laugh. The screaming has loosened him up.

Trees What about you then? Your ex?

Flaps She's worse than a Hobbit. She's a fucking nightmare.

Trees What about your son?

Flaps I don't see him much. She makes it difficult. Conditions. Supervision. All that bollocks.

Trees Why?

Flaps She went off with my best mate. Ex-best mate. I smashed them up. The house and him.

Trees Natural reaction.

Flaps Exactly. Unfortunately, the judge didn't agree. I had a bad time in Afghan on my last tour. (*Beat.*) I wasn't the easiest bugger in the world to live with. What about you?

Trees I'm between relationships right now.

Flaps Taking a breather.

Trees From all the –

Flaps Hobbits knocking at your door.

Trees Beating my door down, more like.

They sir.

Dad's getting dementia. My sister escaped. She's having a life. (*Revealing in confidence.*) I've got some confidence

issues. But apart from that, I'm living the dream. (*Beat.*)
I *have* got Asperger's by the way. That wasn't a lie. Only
mildly. I just find it difficult to process feelings. Emotions.
What about you?

Flaps The play's getting me out of the house. Nothing
else going on. Apart from my treatment. And my bike. I'll
take you out for a ride if you like.

Trees Don't like motorbikes. What treatment?

Flaps EMDR.

Trees What's that?

Flaps Empty Mouth Demands Resupply.

Trees What?

Flaps I'm joking. (*She doesn't laugh.*) Eye Movement
Desensitization and Reprocessing.

Trees You got PTSD?

Flaps Yeah. It's getting better though. Slowly.

Trees My father saw stuff in the Falklands. He never
talks about it though.

Flaps Will he come and see the play?

Trees He's a bit wobbly but I hope so.

*Flaps surprises her by kissing her on the cheek. She
touches her face.*

FOUR

*The cast make the rehearsal room again, and everyone
watches TC as he reads from a piece of A4 paper.*

TC My shift had just started. (*Not reading the next bit.
He confirmes a few facts with his audience.*) At Bastion

my job was to maintain the Chinooks for the Special Forces. (*Reading again.*) I'd just got my mug of coffee and got into the tent. Logged on my laptop. Taken a sip. The flap opened. My son, Darren, had given me the mug. (*He holds up the actual mug.*) This Flight Lieutenant said, 'You have to come with me.' So I got up and I put my coffee down and I followed him to the Chinook. He said, 'You'll have to come with, we're short.' I said, 'What d'you mean, short?' He said, 'We only have one loader and no engineer.' (*He looks up again from his piece of paper to tell them.*) A normal crew is two pilots, two loaders and an engineer. I'm an engineer. (*Back to the story.*) 'But I haven't been up in one of these things for years. I haven't had the necessary . . .' He interrupted me. 'I don't care, Sergeant, you're coming along. It'll only be a couple of hours. In and out.' (*He looks up to tell them.*) They normally fly as a pair, but this was different. Unusual. Only the one Chinook. (*Reading again.*) Within a few minutes we came under fire. Tracer rounds. Small arms and we took evasive action, rocking all over the place. I just started firing. But I was shaking. I took my hand away, but I couldn't stop it shaking. I couldn't breathe. We banked but dropped very low. We'd been hit. The hydraulics had gone. We weren't going to make it. Down we went. Into the ground. Soft ground. Marshes. Smacking all over the place. Electrics hissing. How no one died was a miracle. But we had to get out in case it went up. There was still fuel on board. And we waited, and waited. But no one came. There was only an hour of darkness left. We were sitting ducks. I had a pistol, I wondered whether I would have the courage to use it. Praying the Taliban wouldn't find us first. And I thought of my mug of coffee. And the picture on it of me smiling with Darren. And the words: 'Greatest dad ever, in the history of the world.' And I thought, what the hell am I doing here? We got back to Bastion, and there was laughing and joking, and relief, and I know that's the gallows humour and all. But I just couldn't. I couldn't join in this time. I couldn't. (*Beat.*) How was that, Harry? Is that the sort of thing you're looking for? I'm sorry it's not more . . . IEDs and that.

Len enters with Beth.

Jacko Eh up.

Woody The prodigal returns.

Len I'm delighted to say that Beth has –

Beth Behaved like a bit of plonker. So, I'd like to apologise. I've had a chat with Mags and I'd like to come back if I may.

Woody, Rickshaw, Flaps and Jacko make a joking 'I don't know if that's going to be acceptable' face.

Beth And you lot can shut up for a start.

Woody We've all bonded now.

Jacko Got ppparts and that.

Maggie No we haven't.

Rickshaw The only part left going is the back end of a tank.

Woody With Flaps.

Harry Course you're welcome back, Beth. We're sharing stories.

Beth I know. I'm way ahead of you. (*Rolls out a long speech.*)

James Oh no. It's tome alone.

Beth (*reading*) Last time Gav came home after a long deployment, I didn't want to meet him in the kitchen with the kettle, the TV, the dog and the kids . . . I wanted to meet him half way.

Flaps In Middle Earth.

The women are vocal in telling Flaps to shut up. The guys laugh.

Beth Thank you. Just the two of us. To reconnect. And I had this picture in my head. His homecoming. How it used to be. *Officer and a Gentleman* mixed with *Top Gun.* So, I booked into the Radisson. The Honeymoon Suite.

All the women say 'Ahh'.

Tanya I had my engagement party there.

Sophie So did I. It's lovely.

The boys led by Woody are mocking.

Harry Okay.

Beth I wanted it to be romantic. Had my hair and nails done. My bits waxed.

James Brazilian?

Beth Hollywood.

James No landing strip.

Woody pretends to gag.

Beth And I'm there. The dress he loves. Silky underwear from Agent Provocateur. To welcome him – body and soul.

All the women react

The new fragrance from Thierry Mugler. Proseco. I had the soundtrack from *Fifty Shades of Grey.* The classy bit. And I'm lying there and I'm waiting. And waiting.

There's a knock at the door. And it's not Gav. It's the hotel manager, saying Gav's had a few too many and gone for a curry with the lads.

There is a reaction to this story.

Harry Well, that could be an interesting scene.

Woody You and the manager?!

Beth You're joking. I'm not getting my kit off. Not without sunbeds.

Tanya Now you're talking.

Harry I don't know. We'll have to ask Len.

Maggie Len?

Len (*he starts going through his big file of papers*) What?

Maggie Sunbeds, Len?

James Don't tell us. There's a form.

Woody Look, where are we going with all this?

Maggie It's important for them to know what it's like for us as well. Not just for you.

Woody It wasn't exactly a barrel of laughs out there, you know.

Sophie Yes, we know. We live with it as much as you do. Trying to hold it all together.

Rickshaw We're not slapping on Factor Fifty and lying around on sun-loungers.

James Well, not all the time.

Flaps That's the Paras for you.

Rickshaw Leave the real work to the Marine.

Woody All their Gucci kit.

Hoarse 'Gucci, Gucci, Gucci!'

Woody (*to Beth*) What happened next? It was just getting to the good part. Did he come around later knocking at your back door?

Maggie Oh please!

Beth No he didn't coming knocking at my back door! Actually, I'd prefer he did all that other stuff before coming back.

Trees What do you mean?

Beth You know . . . all that bagging off.

Trees Not prostitutes and that?

Beth Whatever he's got to do, love.

Maggie You don't mean that, Bethany.

Beth I'd rather not know about it, thank you very much. As long as he uses protection.

Maggie I can't believe that.

Beth What happens on deployment stays on deployment.

Maggie You can't mean that. You wouldn't have written that.

Beth Why not? It's just realistic. Course I don't *want* him to knock up some bird in Brazil. Or have some kid turn up on our doorstep and say 'Hello, Dad'.

Maggie tries to interrupt.

But Mags, have you ever asked yourself why you've been married *and* divorced from two military men?

Maggie But you can't live your life without –

Trees Honesty.

Maggie Exactly.

Sophie And loyalty.

Beth If you want to bury your head in fantasy and ideals that's fine. I'm just being practical.

Sophie Practical?!

Beth Realistic.

Hoarse Says the woman whose married a Hobbit.

Maggie And is that how your marriage works?

Beth No one's pulling any wool over my eyes.

Maggie I don't believe you really mean that.

Beth I know where I stand, that's all.

Maggie It's just wrong. (*Beat.*) It's wrong.

Tom The real problem with sunbeds is that when the men do go off on deployment their wives go out on the town, and you can see the mark left on their wedding finger. Where they've taken their ring off?

The women react negatively to this. The men are vocal in supporting Tom.

As a Platoon Commander I had to deal with it all the time. 'Sir, sir, Nobby's been having it off with my missus while I've been on a course.'

Hoarse (*suddenly stands up and advances towards the women*) See! All you women are just slags. (*To Sal.*) And you dykes are even worse!

This causes mayhem as Sal jumps on Hoarse's back. All the others are up, either trying to break up the ensuing argument/fight or joining in.

We hear the opening piano chords to 'Truth is a Beautiful Thing' by London Grammar. Everyone goes into slow motion under the music. Harry goes off after Maggie.

45

Maggie Am I being naive? I wanted a partner who was . . . Was that unrealistic of me?

Harry I don't know.

Maggie Sorry. I didn't mean to make it all about me.

Harry I don't think it's unrealistic.

Maggie Both my husbands were unfaithful, so I suppose I am being naive. I was very young the first time. We couldn't have kids. So, I suppose it was inevitable he'd go off. But my second husband, Phil . . . that was different. I thought he would be the one. He was Bomb Disposal. And we had Cameron. Which was a miracle. But I suppose you have to have a screw loose. Both of you. To do that job.

Harry How do you have a relationship with someone who defuses bombs for a living?

Maggie (*beat*) There's thousands of ticking time bombs walking around out there, Harry. How do you defuse all them? They're back. But they're not really back in here, are they? They're not normal, any of them. Not any more. What they've seen and done. It was hard as a wife. It's even harder as a mother.

She goes back into the rehearsal room.
The lights fade on Harry contemplating what he has let himself in for.

FIVE
LINES OF COMMUNICATION

There is laughter from the group.

Sophie Simon Cowell said no. (*Group reaction of 'ahhh'.*) But I nearly got a yes from Cheryl. She said maybe with a bit more confidence, which is why I signed up for this.

Harry Yeah, not quite sure how that would fit into our play.

Jacko I don't know. Hoarse playing Sharon Osborne?

Harry No, come on. Tell me more about Donny? How hard it is with Donny away so much.

Sophie What do you want me to say?

Harry (*reading from his file*) Making all the decisions without him, because you don't want to worry him. (*Reading another quote.*) The things they miss. Carrying it all on your own.

Sophie I don't think I want that in the play.

James Why not?

Sal She doesn't need to explain.

Harry Sophie. I want this to be a safe place. It's why we're all here. Let's just try something, okay? Trust me. You're getting the kids ready for school. James, you be one of the kids? Sal? Tanya? Kids as well. The phone goes, it's Donny. You haven't heard from him for a couple of weeks.

Sophie Months.

Harry Okay, months. And it comes, just at the wrong time. (*Points to the kitchen.*) You're in the kitchen, packed lunches on the table. Kids arguing.

> *Sophie goes to an area marked out by Harry. Tanya, Sal and James go there as well, and start pretending to be children of about six and seven.*

Sophie Okay. Right. Time for school. Who's ready?

James (*sticking his hand straight up in the air*) Me! Me! / Me!

Tanya (*sticking her hand up higher*) I'm ready, Mummy.

Sal Ow! She hit me.

Tanya I didn't hit you.

Sal Yes, you did.

Tanya No, I didn't.

Sophie Alright, alright. Calm / down.

Sal I don't want to go to school.

James I do.

Sophie Well, you have to.

James I'll have her crisps if she doesn't want / them.

Sal He can't have my crisps –

Tanya That's not fair.

She hits Sal.

Sal Ow!!

Sophie Tanya! Stop it.

Sal hits Tanya back and pulls her hair.

Sal Mummy!

Sophie Will you two stop it right now?!

James I'm hungry and I want spaghetti.

He starts hitting the floor, and chanting 'spaghetti'.
Tanya provokes Sal and they start fighting.

Sophie I said stop it.

Sal Ow! Fucking hell Tanya!

Harry (*intervening and pulling Tanya off Sal*) Hey, hey, hey!

48

Sal Bloody hell!

Tanya (*coming out of the impro*) Sorry. Sorry, everyone.

Harry Full marks for authenticity, Tanya, but let's make the focus on the phone call, okay?

Sophie But that's what it would be like.

Beth Kids running wild.

Sophie Mayhem.

Harry Okay. So, there's mayhem in the kitchen, the phone rings. Jacko, can you be on the other end of the phone.

Jacko What?

Sophie You be Donny. You're somewhere in the Indian Ocean.

Jacko gets up and goes to the opposite side.

Jacko What do I say?

Harry Whatever comes into your mind.

Rickshaw Don't say that.

Harry Don't overthink it.

Rickshaw No danger of that.

Harry Okay, here we go. 'Ring, ring. Ring, ring.'

Sophie (*pretends to pick up a phone*) Hello, Don. Donny?

James, Tanya and Sal make a lot of noise over the top of the phone call.

Sophie Kids, it's Daddy.

James Daddy! I want to speak to / Daddy.

Tanya No, I'm speaking / to Daddy.

Sal Daddy! My Daddy.

Sophie Be quiet please. You can speak to him in a minute. (*Into the pretend phone.*) Don. you alright? Where are you?

Jacko I'm on a ship.

She struggles to hear what he is saying.

Sophie Kids, please! I can't hear your father.

Jacko I'm on a ship.

Sophie You're on a what?

Jacko I'm on a ship.

Sophie Where?

Jacko What?

Sophie Where are you?

Jacko I'm on a ship.

Rickshaw (*stands up*) He's on a fucking ship!

Sophie (*impatient with the kids – it feels very real*) Kids, please!

James I want to speak to Daddy.

Sal No, I'm speaking to Daddy.

Tanya Why should you get to speak to Daddy?

James I've done a brilliant picture / Daddy.

Tanya When are you coming / home?

Sal Daddy? Daddy?

James Is Daddy coming / home?

Sophie (*shouting*) Will you all just shut up! (*Taking the imaginary phone out of the kitchen.*) I need to talk to you, Don. Can you call back? When the kids are at school?

James No!

Tanya I want to speak to Daddy!

Sal No, I'm speaking to him.

Jacko I can't love, sorry. This is it. Can I speak to the kids?

Sophie But I've got so many things to tell you.

James (*pulling the imaginary phone away from Tanya*) Daddy!

Tanya That's not fair. Mummy!

Sal I want to speak to Daddy. When's it my turn?

James Let me speak to Daddy!

Sophie STOP IT! ALL OF YOU! JUST STOP IT!

She pulls away from James, Tanya and Sal. She comes out of the impro, and tries to stop crying.

I'm sorry. I'm so sorry. That's exactly what it's like.

There is underscoring from the beginning of London Grammar's 'Truth is a Beautiful Thing' until the vocal comes in.

Jacko Sorry.

Sophie No it's fine. I'll be fine. That's exactly what it's like. (*She's right back in it, in a panic.*) Our youngest was ill. I didn't know what to tell him. To worry him. She needed an operation. I didn't know what to do.

Images of soldiers coming home and surprising their loved ones fills the screen. We hear the first verse and chorus of 'Truth is a Beautiful Thing'. The company dance. It fades and the cast leave to the sides of the stage.

TC is playing the guitar. Harry watches him. TC stops when he realises he is being watched. Jacko hovers.

Harry That's terrific, TC. I didn't know you played?

TC Keyboards. Guitar. Bit of sax. I was in a band for a while.

Harry (*looking at his file*) You were in a band?

TC Yeah.

Harry Called?

TC No Comment.

Harry Sorry.

TC No, that was the name of the band.

Harry Why didn't you put that on your form?

TC I did.

Harry (*looking more closely at TC's form, and finding 'No Comment'*) Ah. Right. Yup. No comment.

TC (*he gets up to go, stops*) You shouldn't have done that, Harry. You said it was a safe place.

He goes. Harry contemplates. Jacko puts stuff away at the end of the rehearsal day.

Harry Everything okay?

Jacko Can I ask you something?

Harry Course.

Jacko Do you think I could *be* an actor?

Harry You are an actor.

Jacko No, I mean a real actor. Ppprofessional.

Harry (*this stops him from packing up*) Gosh. Um.

Jacko Have I got what it takes?

Harry I don't know, Jacko. That's not for me to say.

Jacko Why not? You're doing it.

Harry Used to.

Jacko You must have some idea. Be honest. I just need to know. It's just . . . It feels right. In here. Something happens.

Harry Well.

Jacko When I'm doing it, I don't –

Harry Stutter.

Jacko If you think I could do it . . . I'd like to fffind out.

Harry Then read. Plays. See films. Different genres.

Jacko Different what? (*He gets a pen and paper.*)

Harry Genres. Types and styles of story.

Jacko Genres.

Harry Yup.

Jacko Would you help me?

Harry Of course.

Jacko nods and thinks as he leaves the rehearsal room.

Jacko Genres.

Harry (*calling back to Jacko*) Get studying, Jacko.

Blackout. Rickshaw is on his mobile phone on another part of the stage. He is holding a cuddly toy – it's a green dragon.

Rickshaw Paula, I know you're there, cos I just see you go in.

Please, Please Paula? Pick up the phone. (*Sees the curtains move.*) I just seen the curtain (*Trails off.*) How's the kids? I didn't realise he was Lacey's dad. I thought you was . . . It's stupid I know. It's the medication, it ain't me. You know that. I'd never hurt you. You're the most important thing in the world. You and the kids. Please, love. I can't bear this. Call me back. I'm doing this thing now, as part of my rehab. I want to tell you about it. (*He drops the cuddly toy on the floor.*)

Blackout.

Sophie (*calling to the other room, off*) Don? Donny?

She takes off her coat and bag, and picks up the cuddly toy.
Donny (Jacko) comes on. He has a can of beer in his hand. We hear the kids, the dog and a TV off.

Donny (*to the offstage kids*) Hey kids, Mummy's home.

Sophie What have you been doing?

Donny What do you mean?

Sophie I go out for a few hours and it looks like a bomb's hit the place.

Donny (*upbeat mood punctured*) Where have you been?

Sophie I told you I was going out.

Donny No you didn't.

Sophie Donny, I did.

Donny Not this fucking long.

Sophie Don't use that language Don –

Donny Fucking off / like that without telling me.

Sophie In front of / the kids.

Donny Where you been?

Sophie Didn't you give the kids their tea?

Donny Don't criticise / me!

Sophie I'm not criticizing / you.

Donny You should have been here, Soph.

Sophie Have the kids not eaten?

Donny I'm feeding them, alright.

Sophie They should have been fed ages ago.

Donny Look, if you don't like the way I do / things –

Sophie They've got their routine.

Donny I know they've got their routine.

Sophie Then why are they eating now? They should be bathed and ready for bed.

Donny Well you should have been here then, shouldn't you?!

Sophie I can't be here twenty-four seven.

Donny Why not? I am.

Sophie Don't be ridiculous.

Donny Why am I being ridiculous?

Sophie It's your choice to stay inside, Don.

Donny It's not my choice.

Sophie It doesn't matter.

Donny No, come on then? Why am I being ridiculous?

Sophie I said it doesn't matter. I'll deal with it.

She tries to go past Donny towards the offstage kitchen. He stops her by the arm.

Donny Where have you been then?

Sophie I told you, I was going out to rehearsals.

Donny What rehearsals?

Sophie For the play.

Donny What play?

Sophie I told you, Don. I'm doing this play.

Donny What? Why?

Sophie What do you mean 'Why?' Because I want to.

Donny Oh right. And bollocks to everyone else then is / it?

Sophie Look, I'm not going to have this conversation now.

Donny All your new actory friends?!

Sophie It's not like that, Donny.

Donny (*imitating her*) 'Oh, it's not like that, Donny.'

Sophie (*anger rising*) No.

She gets free of Donny and heads towards the sound of the children, off.

Donny 'Thanks, Donny, for helping out. Oh that's alright, Soph. I did my best. But obviously it wasn't good enough.' I'm just in the fucking way. I know that alright.

Donny throws his beer can at the back wall. Explosion.

SIX
STANDING ORDERS

The cast come back on and sit down in chairs at the back. Tom stands up and walks with his stick to the middle and puts his hand gently on Jacko's (Donny's) shoulder. Jacko gets up and goes back to his chair, dazed.

Tom I'd like to tell you about Lance Corporal Robbie Douglas if I may. I was Robbie's Commanding Officer when the first Battalion was deployed on Herrick Twelve. (*Clears his throat. Starts to read.*) Robbie saved my life on a patrol, one swelteringly hot, fidgety afternoon in Helmand. He was just one of those men. Kind. Brave. Mischievous. (*Looking up.*) You didn't want to be anywhere near our Rabs or Lance Corporal Hennessy on April Fools' Day. The Ant and Dec of Bravo Company. (*Reading.*) In September last year, I found myself at the National Arboretum. Robbie took his own life a year and ten days after we returned from Afghanistan, and a year after that we'd gathered together, family, company, regiment, to remember Robbie. Robbie's mum, Janice, had asked me to read a poem. And Lance Corporal Hennessy had written a speech. Not natural orators, either of us. (*Looking up.*) Neither of us Benedict Cumberbatch if you know what I mean. But it was important. And I just want to share the poem with you, because it made me realise I should thank my lucky stars and all that.

His laughter was better than birds in the morning.

His smile turned the wind . . .

He *drops the piece of paper, struggles to pick it up. Under his breath: 'Bugger.'*

As I said, not a natural orator. Actually . . . Um . . . When I knew the ceremony was going to be at least an hour. Well, it's an awfully long time when you've got a prostate problem. Call of the lavatory and so forth. So that morning, I went into Charlotte's – that's my daughter, I went into her room and um, I requisitioned one of her . . . her um . . . sanitary towels. I wanted to be on the safe side. A contingency plan. Anyway, just before the ceremony, I popped into the gents to apply the aforementioned contingency object. Rather tricky little things. And I could hear Lance Corporal Hennessy pacing up and down by the sinks, going over his speech. Pages of the stuff. I heard a lot of expletives. Came out of the cubicle tapped him on the shoulder, to be honest, I snapped a bit, and told him to pull himself together – you see, I'd learnt my poem, so it was a different kettle of fish. (*Beat.*) We were outside. Warm, cloudless afternoon. Packed. And as I got to the end of the poem, I looked down to get a bit of a grip, and I saw that I had wet myself. And it was spreading. So, I couldn't step away from the lectern. I was trapped. I had nothing to hide the evidence. One doesn't remove one's hat, you see. Not outside. And I froze. Suddenly, Lance Corporal Hennessey was walking towards me, and he stopped, expecting me to give way to him. But I stood my ground, he immediately saw the problem. Without a moment's thought he handed me the sheets of paper, his speech, which I used to cover myself as I walked back. My camouflage. And I carried on walking, all the time I could hear Lance Corporal Hennessey stumbling his way through without his script. Buggering on regardless. And I walked all the way back to the cubicle. Cleaned myself up. And I cried. I'd like to say it was for Robbie, and all the others, but actually . . . it was Lance Corporal Hennessey . . . his kindness . . . It caught me off guard.

The company sing 'Soldier On'

Soldier On Anthem

When the dark descends on you.
And a smile hides despair.
When the lights don't shine on you,
And it all feels unfair.

When it's all too much for you,
And no one is there.
When the world's lost touch with you,
And it's too much to bear.

We will endeavour to,
Turn back the tide.
With heads together, we'll
Be right by your side.

We will be there for you
To catch you if you fall.
Shine a light if it's dark for you,
All for one and one for all.

Let go of yesterday,
Of all the things you've seen and done.
Let go what others say,
And together, we will Soldier On.

As the music finishes and they put Tom back down on the ground, the final moment is Tom, using all his effort to come to attention. Blackout.

End of Part One.

Part Two

The introduction to 'Titanium' by David Guetta starts to play. Under it, we hear famous quotes, including Colonel Tim Collins: 'We are going into Iraq to liberate not to conquer . . . as for the others I expect you to rock their world'; John Nott and Margaret Thatcher: 'Just rejoice at that news and congratulate our forces and the Marines.'

SEVEN
THE SEVEN P'S

PRIOR PLANNING AND PREPARATION
PREVENTS A PISS-POOR PERFORMANCE

The auditorium of a large theatre is projected on the back wall. A mirror image, except for the fact that all the seats are empty. It should feel vast and scary. All the cast, except for Harry, Len and James start coming on to the stage.

Woody Fuck me! That is big.

Jacko That is very big.

Rickshaw I think we can all agree that this is very big.

Trees Oh my God.

Sal Wow!

Sophie Oh my God.

Jacko (*enjoying it; holding an imaginary mic*) Hello, Wembley!

Tom Impressive, isn't it?

Tanya Imagine that full.

Trees I'd rather not.

Flaps I think I'm going to be sick.

Maggie We've sung in bigger places than this.

Beth Twickenham. Albert Hall.

Flaps Alright. Betty big bollocks.

Beth Just saying. It's not that bad.

Flaps Unfortunately, for us stage virgins, it's a bit 'crap your pants' time.

Woody I've got that same squitty feeling you get in –

Rickshaw In a contact?

Jacko Alan Snack Bar pumping the tracer down. (*To Beth and Maggie.*) BANG!

Rickshaw RPG rounds.

Woody Nothing like it.

Rickshaw Smell of cordite.

Flaps Do you mind? I'm trying to have a panic attack over here.

Rickshaw (*taking a photo*) My little girl would love all this. She won't believe I'm doing a play. (*Pulling Jacko into a selfie.*)

Jacko (*to Rickshaw*) You couldn't lend us a few quid till the end of the month could you? Till my pppension lands.

Beth Got a hot tip then, have you?

Jacko Mind your own business. It's for research.

Beth Yeah, right.

Len comes on to the stage and suddenly stops.

Len Listen in! Jesus fucking H Christ!

Woody Oi, language, Lennard.

Len I know but look at it.

Harry comes on. Excited.

Tom Come on, Len. Pull yourself together, man.

Len Yeah, but it's, it's, it's, it's –

Harry dumps a big pile of scripts on the floor. It's as if they've just heard a loud bang.

Flaps Do you mind, Harry!

Harry God. Sorry.

Jacko Loud bbbbangs, Harry.

Harry Absolutely. Sorry.

Jacko It's not . . . it's not . . . it's not . . . FUCK!!

He goes for Harry.

It's not cool, Harry.

Woody (*stopping Jacko from hitting his head*) Hey, hey, hey.

Len Alright everybody. Let's not panic. Alright? Whatever you do, don't panic.

Sal (*in Yorkshire accent*) You're not panicking are you, Len?

Sophie Suddenly feels very real, doesn't it?

Tanya Very real.

Len It's very big, Harry. You sure about this?

Harry Well. We work as a team, we rehearse.

Tom Don't bump into the furniture.

Tanya What furniture?

Harry Ah yes. Now I don't suppose anyone here's read *The Empty Space* by Peter Brook?

Hoarse I have.

Harry Really?

Hoarse No.

Harry Well, that, ladies and gentlemen, is our script.

He focuses everyone's attention to the pile of scripts.

Maggie You've done it?

Harry Hot off the press. All your stories.

Sophie (*going to the pile of scripts*) Can we?

Harry Tuck in.

They all take scripts and excitedly look at them. The following dialogue overlaps and tumbles out. Tom is the last to reach down for a script.

Rickshaw Guess who's got the first line? –

Flaps What? Why does he get the first line? –

Sophie (*to Sal*) We're singing. –

Sal Oh my God! Where? –

Trees Shakespeare!? –

Harry No, it's a reference to –

Sophie Look. Taylor Swift. –

Sal You've got to be kidding! –

Harry Only if you want to. We don't have to. If it's going to –

Tom suddenly falls over as he tries to pick up his script. TC and Hoarse are the first ones to help him. Hoarse gets a chair. TC helps Tom up.

Tanya Tom!

Sal What is it, Tom?

Hoarse You alright, sir?

Tom Please don't call me sir. Christ! How many more times?!

Hoarse Sorry.

Tom No, I'm sorry.

TC It's alright. I've got you, Tom.

Sal goes to get him a glass of water.

Len Everything okay, Tom?

Tom (*angry with himself*) Well that's a bloody stupid question. Clearly everything is not okay. Okay?

Len Okay.

Tom Sorry.

Harry Don't be silly.

Tom No, I'm sorry to make such a fuss. Bloody thing just won't work. I feel such a fool.

Harry Well, don't.

There is a chorus of agreement.

Woody Yeah, we got Flaps doing that –

Rickshaw He doesn't need any help –

Tom (*to Len and Harry*) Actually, Harry, I'm really sorry to do this to everyone, but I'm afraid I just don't think I'm going to be able to carry on.

Harry Nonsense. You'll be fine Tom. / Honestly. I've written –

Tom No Harry. Not this time / I'm afraid.

Harry We'll get you up / and running

Tom Didn't you just hear me, man? I said no.

There is an uncomfortable silence. Sal comes back with a small bottle of water.

Sal Here you go, Tom.

Tom (*taking the bottle*) Thanks. (*Drinks with an unsteady hand.*)

They are all stung by this news. Tom starts to limp off helped by TC and Hoarse.

I can manage, thank you.

The others watch him. Everyone is deflated.

Harry Maybe when you're feeling better, we could talk about something behind the scenes?

Tom I'll think about it.

Len Alright, so, we've lost Tom, but there is some good news to announce . . . On your feet, Harry?

Harry Yes. Not sure this is quite the right time, Len.

Len Every cloud, Harold.

Harry Through a regimental contact of Len's, we've secured the involvement of James Blunt.

Len James Blunt.

Sophie James Blunt?

Harry James Blunt.

Len James Blunt.

Sophie As in . . . THE James Blunt?

Maggie In the play?

Harry Yes.

Tanya I think I'm going to faint.

Woody I think I'm going to throw up.

Maggie Oh stop it.

Rickshaw Why?

Maggie Why?! It's James Blunt.

Rickshaw So?!

Tanya What do you mean, so?

Woody So, this whole thing just becomes a PR stunt for James Blunt?

Harry Not at all.

Rickshaw It better not.

Len It'll generate a lot of interest.

Woody I thought this was all about us.

Sophie We want an audience though.

Beth Too bloody right we do. If I'm going to get spotted.

Woody The only people who are going to spot you are the talent police. Have you fucking arrested!

Beth goes for Woody and they have to be separated.

Tanya Leave him. It's not worth it.

Len (*getting upset*) I thought you'd all be pleased.

Maggie We are pleased, Len.

Tanya We are.

Len The strings I've had to pull. I've had to write letters. You have no idea the work that goes in to all this, the logistics and assessments. The worry of who's going to turn up and who's fallen out with who, and Health and Safety. I'm just a bloody Sergeant Major! I don't need any of this crap. (*Turning and seeing what Sal has been doing. He stomps off.*) I don't even like his music.

Beth Len?

Len (*off, pronouncing the 'j'*) Oh, stick it up your junta!

Rickshaw (*after Len has gone, turning to Beth*) I wouldn't worry, he's probably got a form for that.

James has come on. He is now taking the first tentative steps as Jenny, and is dressed as a woman, in shirt and trousers with a bit of make-up. This stops everyone. Jenny walks towards the group and picks up a script.

Rickshaw Fuck me.

James Jenny.

Sal Wow. You look amazing.

Jenny Thank you.

Maggie Doesn't she look amazing?

Jenny It's okay. You don't have to. (*Make a fuss.*)

Beth You do, babe, you do. (*Look amazing.*)

Sophie She does. Amazing.

Jenny It's still me. Okay.

Harry Welcome back. Jenny.

They all welcome Jenny into the group, except for Woody, Hoarse, TC and Tanya.

Jenny Thank you. I'm just trying it out. I'm not there yet.

Suddenly Hoarse barges through everyone and leaves the stage.

Beth Oi!

Sophie Hoarse!

Harry Hoarse?

Hoarse turns around.

Hoarse You should have told us you were going to do this. (*To Harry.*) Did you know he was going to turn up like this?

Jenny It's Jenny.

Hoarse Is it really?

He turns around and starts to go.

Harry Hoarse?

Hoarse (*stops and comes back again*) You should have warned us, that's all.

Sal Why should he have warned us?

Hoarse doesn't know what to say and goes.

Tanya Oh, don't be a twat, Hoarse.

Rickshaw Come back, mate.

Jenny It's alright, okay? I'd rather you didn't, you know?

Woody Look, for the record . . . not everyone is totally cool with this.

Jenny I'm not asking you to be. Any of you.

There is a chorus of admonishment towards Woody.

Woody What? Just saying. You just need to give some of us bootnecks time. That's all.

Jenny I know.

There is an awkward pause.

Woody Personally, I'm totally comfortable with guys dressing up as girls. We do it all the time.

Rickshaw All the time.

Jenny (*provoking*) And I am RAF Regiment so what do you expect? (*Beat.*) Right. So, any tips?

Woody Yeah. Not sure about the hair thing.

Jenny gives Sal a decorative hair clip. They exit while offering tips on make-up. The tips tumble out.

Beth Ignore him, babe, he hasn't got a clue.

Sophie I've got a foundation colour that'll really match.

Jenny I used to wear make-up on exercise, but it was a lot more slapdash.

Flaps (*singing*) Cos your beautiful.

They all shout 'Shut up!'

Blackout.

EIGHT

COLLATORAL DAMAGE

Sal is looking at and fiddling with the small and decorative hair clip in her hand.

Sal Right. Okay. Um. Well, it was while we were waiting for a young marine to come in. Cat A Trauma Call. Medivac, and there's a procedure, you know? We've all got our job to do. And we were prepped and waiting. When suddenly there was just . . . chaos. There'd been a suicide bomber at a local wedding. Multiple casualties. We were overwhelmed. And I was suddenly with this young woman. About twenty, twenty-one. We'd worked on her. She wasn't showing any pain. But I think she knew she was dying. She'd lost too much blood. Internal injuries were just 'catastrophic'. Tension haemothorax. There was nothing we could do . . . I could do. So, I held her hand. Just held her hand as she slipped away. No, she didn't slip away. She died. Okay? She suffocated on her own blood. And we'd cut away what was left of her wedding dress. I picked it up off the floor. She was the bride, you see? It was her wedding day. Her name was Afarin, which means 'Praise be'. It was supposed to be Afarin's wedding day. And her wedding dress was elegant and . . . beautiful. And I took this from her hair. I didn't mean to keep it. I put it in my pocket . . . to keep it safe, I didn't realise it was still there. I saw so many casualties and deaths, and you learn to cope with it. You cope, and you move on. You do your job. You shut off. You all pull together. And you move on. But it's her, it's Afarin, it's always her I go back to. Sorry. Can we stop?

The actors make a hotel bedroom and Sophie and Donny's living room. Two single beds, and a neon sign outside the bedroom window. Donny is crouched in a dark corner, watching Sophie. We cut between the two rooms.

Sophie Don? (*She doesn't see him.*) Donny?

She doesn't take her coat off. Eating fish and chips. She sits.

Flaps and Trees in a hotel room.

Trees It's a twin.

Flaps Yup.

Trees Why did you get a twin?

Flaps It's all they had.

Trees (*sarcastic*) Great.

Donny Nice, are they?

Sophie (*surprised*) Jeezuz, Donny! What you doing down there?

Flaps We can push them together?

Trees Alright.

Sophie I said I'd get fish and chips. (*Still no reply.*)

Flaps and Trees go and push the two single beds together.

Sophie Don? You okay? (*No reply.*)

Flaps That's alright.

Sophie At least have a chip?

Trees I need to be on the other side.

Donny Yeah.

Flaps Okay.

They change sides. Flaps tries to break the ice. Sophie goes over to Donny.

Sophie Don? (*Reaching out to him.*)

Flaps Do you come here often?

Trees Bed's too soft.

Flaps You can lie on me if you want.

Sophie Donny?

Trees Was it expensive?

Flaps I got a deal. (*He tries to put his arm around her.*)

Donny What?

Trees This feels weird.

Flaps Why?

Sophie Talk to me.

Trees A hotel in Havant.

She gets off the bed and goes to the window.

I only live over there.

Flaps It's romantic.

She turns and looks out of the window.

Sophie There's guys there like you, Don.

Donny What do you mean, like me?

Sophie Who've got what you've got.

Donny And what have I got?

Flaps gets off the bed and goes and stands behind Trees at the window.

Donny What do you know about PTSD?

Sophie They talk, Don.

Donny Really know.

Flaps (*tender and tentative*) Teressa's a lovely name.

Trees No, it's not.

Sophie No, you're right. I don't know.

Donny What are you telling them –

Sophie Nothing –

Donny About me?

Sophie Keep your voice / down.

Donny Our stuff is private for fuck sake.

Sophie Be quiet, you'll wake the kids.

Flaps Shall I put the telly on?

Donny And these are fucking disgusting.

As he gets more agitated, he throws the fish and chips against a wall.

Sophie Right.

Donny Fucking horrible. Soggy, fucking / chips.

Sophie Don, stop it.

Donny Fucking waste of time.

Sophie suddenly completely loses it, and throws the fish and chips all over him.

Sophie That's it. Alright? I don't care. Okay? Poisonous fucking stone cold chips. I don't care!

Donny (*surprised*) Alright! Calm down. will ya?

Sophie I don't care.

Donny Alright.

Sophie I don't fucking care!

Donny It's only fish and chips.

Sophie No, it isn't only fucking fish and chips.

Donny I'm sorry. Alright?

Sophie (*regaining her calm*) That's what it's like, Don. Living with you. All the time. So, don't tell me I don't know anything about PTSD. Okay? Or the kids.

> *He turns away. Trees and Flaps are still looking out of the window.*

Flaps Good view up here, innit.

Trees I can literally see my house.

Flaps Everyone in their bubbles. Getting on with their lives. Don't worry about your dad, he'll be alright.

Trees How do you know?

Flaps He will. You put him to bed. You'll be back first thing.

> *Donny goes to Sophie. He tries to put a sympathetic arm on her shoulder, but she is too wounded to respond, and shrugs off his arm.*
>
> *Trees turns around and looks at Flaps. He tries to kiss her softly. But she moves away, and picks up a card with the phone number of the hotel on it.*

Flaps What you doing?

Trees I'll text my dad the number.

Flaps Why?

Trees Just in case.

Flaps He's fast asleep. You'll wake him up.

Trees He won't wake up.

Flaps Well then.

He starts taking off his shoes. She freezes.

Trees What are you doing?

Flaps Getting comfortable.

Trees Why?

Flaps What do you mean, why?

Trees What are you planning?

Trees suddenly runs out and goes, leaving Flaps at a complete loss.

Flaps Where you going? Trees? Where are you going?

*Sophie and Donny come together for a hug.
We hear 'Nightminds' by Missy Higgins and they dance.*

NINE
DECOMPRESSION . . . ?'

Maggie's house. Cameron is in uniform with his kit. She screams with surprise. She throws her arms around him.

Maggie Cameron!

Cameron Mum! Eh! Mum! Give us a chance.

Maggie You're here. I can't believe it.

Cameron Mum! You're doing my back in.

Maggie I missed you so much. I can't believe you're finally here.

Cameron I'm not going away, you can relax alright.

Maggie Look at you. So handsome. I can't believe it. You look like a film star. Why didn't you tell me? I was going to come to meet you. I made a banner and everything.

Cameron That's exactly why I didn't tell you.

Maggie I had it all planned.

Cameron Mum?

Maggie Let me look at you. You've grown.

Cameron No I haven't.

Maggie You have. Another inch at least.

Cameron (*coming forward and getting a small box out of his rucksack*) I got you this.

Maggie Oh Cam. (*She's very touched.*)

Cameron You don't know what it is yet. Open it.

Maggie (*takes the box, opens it, and takes out an expensive necklace*) It's beautiful. It must have cost a fortune. Oh my God they are. They're real. You shouldn't have done it Cam.

Cameron I wanted to. The stones are local. An ancient setting made for a Babylonian queen.

Maggie Babylonian queen. Put it on me.

He puts the necklace around her neck and fastens it.

Cameron Hold still.

He is slightly behind Maggie as they look out into an imaginary mirror.

Maggie Oh Cam. It's beautiful. I love it.

She turns round and hugs him.

Thank you. I wish you'd let me come and meet you.

Cameron Chrissy met me.

Maggie Chrissy?

Cameron Yeah.

Maggie (*surprised but trying hard to hide her hurt*)
Oh, right.

Cameron She dropped me.

Maggie She dropped you?

Cameron She's parking up.

Maggie (*doesn't know how to take this*) She didn't say
anything.

Cameron I asked her not to.

Maggie Why would you do that?

Cameron I proposed. I proposed to Chrissy and she said
yes. Can you believe it? I wanted to do it as soon as we
landed. I had it all planned. Rehearsed it with the lads.
I got it on my phone. (*He wants to show her the footage
on his phone.*) I got her the most beautiful ring. Local
diamonds / and an –

Maggie (*not wanting to look at the footage*) – ancient
setting made for a Babylonian queen.

Cameron (*this isn't what he expected*) Princess –

  Maggie says nothing.

Cameron Say something? (*She says nothing.*) Please.

Maggie What do you want me to say?

Cameron Er . . . Congratulations. I'm really pleased for
you. Something like that.

Maggie Cam –

Cameron (*shaking his head*) No.

Maggie You're too young.

Cameron I don't want to hear it.

Maggie Both of you.

Cameron You're not going to change it, Mum, you're not.

Maggie I don't want the same thing to happen to you that happened to me.

Cameron You're jealous. I'm not your baby boy, okay? I love Chrissy and I'm going to marry her.

Maggie Please, Cam.

Cameron Just be happy for me.

Maggie I beg you. Don't rush into this.

Cameron She's never been good enough for you.

Maggie Course she has. Oh, Cam that's / not true.

Cameron Every girlfriend I've ever / had.

Maggie I love Chrissy.

Cameron Truth is you're a sad old woman who drove me dad away because you hated what he did, and now you want to keep me tied to you cos you're scared of being alone. (*Heads to the door.*)

Maggie I'm not scared of being alone. I've just been alone.

Cameron Good. That's alright then.

Maggie Where are you going?

Chrissy (Beth) suddenly appears at the front door.

Chrissy (*bouncy*) Hiya.

Cameron Come on. We're going.

Chrissy What?

Maggie No.

Cameron Yes.

Chrissy Why?

Maggie Please.

Cameron Truth is, Chrissy said you'd be like this.

Chrissy Be like what? No, I didn't. (*Pushing Cameron away.*)

Maggie Don't go love. Please.

Cameron No.

Maggie Stay. Please. (*To Chrissy.*) Tell him.

Chrissy What's happened?

Cameron Why? And listen to you?

Maggie I won't say anything –

Cameron No!

Maggie Wait. Please, Cam. Please!

Cameron picks up his kit and goes.

Chrissy (*doesn't know whether to stay or go*) What happened?

Maggie He told me.

Cameron comes back in.

Cameron (*to Chrissy*) Are you coming?

Chrissy We can't go like this.

Cam tries to go but she pulls him back.

Cam?! Don't spoil everything.

Cameron Me?!

Chrissy Yes. Look at your mum. (*She comforts Maggie.*)

Cameron Don't. Just don't. (*He goes.*)

Chrissy You can't just leave her like this. Cam?

Chrissy looks back at Maggie, then rushes off after Cam. Sal (Paula) sings 'Wings' by Birdy. This underscores her picking up Maggie from the floor. Maggie goes, and Sal stays centre stage while . . .

TEN

FIBUA . . . FIGHTING IN BUILT-UP AREAS

Trees is sitting on a chair. Flaps comes on. She sees him. He sees her. A piano version of 'Wings' continues under.

Flaps What did you do that for?

Trees Sorry.

Flaps I've been looking everywhere.

Trees You didn't have to.

Flaps What did I do wrong?

Trees Nothing.

Flaps Well, I must have done something.

Trees doesn't answer. He is disappointed and confused.

I was worried that's all. (*Puts her bag down by her.*) You left this.

He starts to go.

Trees Wait.

He stops and turns. He waits for an explanation which doesn't come.

Flaps I thought you and me . . . (*could have . . .*)

Silence.

Flaps (*hurt, but trying not to show it*) I'll see you then.

He starts to go.
Trees wants to say 'I do like you', but can't.

Sal sings another verse and chorus of 'Wings'. At the climax of this Rickshaw comes forward out of the shadows with a bunch of flowers. As he touches her shoulder the music stops, and as soon as she sees him she starts walking off.

Rickshaw Don't go. Paula? Wait. Please? Paul.

She stops and turns to him across the space.

Paula What do you want?

Rickshaw I just wanted / to –

Paula What?

Rickshaw (*tries to gives her the flowers*) I got you these.

Paula (*she steps back and won't take them*) Why?

Rickshaw What do you mean, why?

Paula What are you doing, Sean?

Rickshaw How you been?

Paula How do you think?

Rickshaw How the kids?

Paula Still traumatised. Why you here? You know you're not allowed.

Rickshaw Paula –

Paula There's a court order / Sean.

Rickshaw I know –

Paula Five hundred meters.

Rickshaw Five minutes. Please?

Paula I can't, Sean. Not again.

Rickshaw Please.

Paula You can't be here, Sean. I've seen you. Over there in the bushes. Looking. If Lily sees you doing that . . .

She doesn't move. Rickshaw backs away to the other end of the stage.

Rickshaw We've changed the medication. It was the drugs, Paul, not me. That's what made me depressed.

Paula And violent?

Rickshaw And violent. It was the side effects of the / drugs.

Paula What you did. How can I explain? How could you think I was cheating on you?

Rickshaw I know.

Paula He's Lily's friend's dad, for God's sake!

Rickshaw I know.

Paula You beat the crap out of him!

Rickshaw He was looking –

Paula He was trying to HELP!

Silence

(*Incredulous.*) And where would I get the time?

Rickshaw I'm sorry.

Paula You were violent before.

Rickshaw That was always to myself. Never to you or Lily or Barn.

82

Paula Sean, how does a six-year-old or eight-year-old process seeing their daddy hitting his head against a wall? Over and over and over again.

Rickshaw I know. I'm damaged.

Paula You just bottle it all / up.

Rickshaw I am working on it / now Paul.

Paula Would never let me in.

Rickshaw I know.

Paula Any of us.

Rickshaw I didn't know how.

Paula We haven't been a family since before you got back. Sean.

Rickshaw I promise.

Paula Do you know some times I wish you'd been killed over there. (*Beat.*) Then least we could have grieved for you. Remembered you properly. With love. Not like this. Scared of you. What you might do. What's in your eyes.

Rickshaw (*this really hits him and hurts*) I know. I've been having treatment.

Paula Good for you. The kids have been seeing someone too. At school. They're too young to be doing that. And you caused that. You!

Rickshaw It's always there in here. On a loop. I try my best not to focus on it, but sometimes it just . . . And I panic. I can't hold it in. Seeing kids and stuff, same as Lily and Barn.

He takes a deep breath. He is on the edge.
    Silence.

Rickshaw I want to read you something. Can I read you something?

Paula Okay.

Rickshaw gets out a piece of A4 paper he has written on and starts to read

Rickshaw When I was a kid, fourteen, fifteen, I always had this ritual. Summer ritual. The first actual day when it really felt like summer. When the sun really warms up your face and you can smell the first cut of the grass –

Paula I'd sit in my garden, put on the Beach Boys, wear the old straw hat my grandad gave me. I know this story, Sean.

Rickshaw I did that this year. It wasn't long after I got back. Remember? And I just felt numb. I couldn't feel anything. Good or bad. And I went to the top of Jury's Inn. I wrote you a note. (*He goes back to reading again from the piece of A4.*) I bought some pills and a bottle of Jack. Had my medals. My MC. Pathetic. I thought they meant something. I started drinking, opened the pills, but my phone went. I wasn't going to answer it, I thought it was Paula, but something made me look, and it was Dave. My friend, Big Dave. And he said, 'What's wrong fella? I can hear it in your voice?' And I said, 'I'm in trouble Dave, I don't think I can make it.' He said, 'Where are you, kid? I'm coming right over.' And he did. (*He starts to lose it, but struggles on.*) And I'm here. Sometimes I wish I wasn't . . . the only thing that makes me put one foot forward in front of the other every day is my beautiful wife Paula, my daughter Lily and my son Barney, and I'll do whatever I can, fight whatever demons and dragons I've got to fight, to get my way back to them.

He looks to her for something . . . anything.

I'm doing this thing Paul. It's a play. We had to write something . . . that meant something to each of us. I

84

wrote that. It would mean the world to me if you'd come. There's a ticket there.

Paula puts her arms around him in a forgiving hug. 'Wings' swells and finishes. Suddenly Harry is there, watching.

Harry That's beautiful, Rickshaw, and that's exactly how it was?

Rickshaw breaks away from Paula.

Rickshaw Was it fuck?!

He repositions Paula away from him.

Rickshaw She . . . (*Repeating the dialogue.*) I'm doing this thing Paul. It's a play. We had to write something . . . that meant something to each of us. It would mean the world to me if you'd come. There's a ticket there.

Paula goes towards her house. Rickshaw turns around with the flowers. As he goes he passes Trees, who is still in her scene, sitting on a wall. He gives her the flowers and walks away. There is a single shot and Trees fall backwards like she's been shot by a sniper. The rest of the cast, minus Jacko, rush on. This is underscored by music – The Killers track, 'All These Things That I've Done'.

A choreographed dance of stylised violence intensifies. Tom is now the stage manager, along with TC. Sound of battle, helicopters, gunfire. Some kind of ritualised movement.

ELEVEN
NO PLAN SURVIVES CONTACT WITH THE ENEMY

Woody comes out of the scene.

Harry Okay. Stop! Stop! What is it, Woody?

Flaps Come on, mate.

Harry Without Jacko you've got to be there otherwise it doesn't work.

Sal Woody?

Woody I can't.

Tanya What do you mean, you can't?

Rickshaw Oh come on, mate.

Sophie You've got to.

Woody (*shaking his head*) Sorry. No.

Beth Why not?

Len If it's upsetting *you*, think of how the audience is going / to feel –

Woody It's not upsetting me. You think that's upsetting me?

Len Well, it certainly feels like / it's –

Woody It's just crap.

Len Pardon?

Woody It doesn't work.

Len Now you listen to me –

Woody It's shit, Len. It's embarrassing.

Tom Woody!

Sal It's a symbol, okay.

Woody Of what?

Maggie Of fear.

Woody It's shit.

Harry What? Because you say it is?

Woody Yes.

Harry You?

Woody It's clichéd. Embarrassing.

Sal Says who?

Beth Oh for God's sake. The world according to Woody.

Sophie Please, Woody.

Woody (*pointing to Beth*) How does that create fear?

Beth Cos *you've* got, like, a monopoly on anything emotional, haven't you?

Woody Yeah, actually looking at you, you do scare me shitless. No wonder your husband's a Hobbit. He's probably fucking blind as well.

Beth goes for Woody and has to be restrained.

Beth You horrible / bastard!

Harry That's enough. / Please!

Len Woody! –

Woody I think I know something about fear, yes. What it feels like being in a contact.

Harry Calm down.

Woody You have no idea.

Harry No. Exactly.

Woody No idea.

Harry No. I don't know what it's like.

Sophie That's the point surely.

Harry So show us then. Don't just criticise. Come on. Show us.

Woody Back me up, guys. I'm not going to be complicit in 'this'!

Beth What? (*Imitating.*) Cos you've got a condition?' PTSD –

Woody That's right –

Beth Which seems to come and go whenever you need it to –

Woody You don't have a clue, do you? –

Tom (*standing and summoning up all his strength to shout*) THAT'S ENOUGH!

Woody What are we doing here, Harry? Tell me? I feel like an idiot doing this airy-fairy wank! You put a soldier on the stage and that's what you're going to get.

Harry Have you been drinking?

> *This catches Woody off guard. He feels betrayed that none of them can understand. He walks offstage.*

Harry Woody! Woody! Come back here! Don't just bugger off! COME BACK HERE! (*Silence.*) Sorry. Everyone. Beth. (*To himself.*) Damn!

Len And that, I believe, is tea.

> *The rest of the actors disperse. Len goes to Harry.*

Harry How the hell did that happen?

Len Right. That's it. It's better all round if Woody doesn't come back.

Harry No.

Len It's never going to work.

Harry (*impatient*) Maybe he's got a point.

Len Not like that he hasn't. He's unstable.

Harry We can't give up on him. He needs this more than any of them. And where the hell's Jacko? (*To the cast.*) Anyone seen Jacko? Tom?

Tom gets up, dialing on his mobile.

Tom I don't know, I'm afraid.

Harry This is crazy. It's either Jacko, or Woody or . . . Is there anyone else who has somewhere more important they need to be?!

Tom I'll go and make some calls. (*Going.*)

Harry Thank you, Tom.

Len We've left messages at Mike Jackson's.

Tom (*going*) He's not answering his phone again.

Len I think there was a problem with credit.

Harry What?

Len He said he didn't have any money to top up.

Harry Doesn't he get a pension? Benefits?

Len I don't know. He was on the streets till a few months ago.

Harry He hasn't relapsed, has he? (*To the cast.*) Anyone seen Jacko? TC?

TC 'Fraid not. I didn't see him at breakfast either.

The cast are drinking cups of tea, eating cake, and checking their phones.
   Harry crouches in front of a chair with his script file. Beth is still fuming.

Jenny Lovely cake Tanya.

Tanya (*pleased*) Thank you. It's my own recipe. Sea salted gluten free butterscotch dark chocolate brownie, rich with a sumptuous gooeyness.

89

Jenny That's not a cake. It's a work of art.

Sal How's your Cameron doing, by the way?

Maggie Oh you know.

Sophie I hear congratulations are in order.

Maggie (*thinking she means about the engagement*) Oh? Where did you hear that?

Sophie Friend of Donny's knows his Company Sergeant Major. He's just come back as well. He said Cameron's being promoted.

Maggie (*trying to hide her surprise*) Yeah. That's right. He is. Yeah.

   Tom comes back on. He goes to Harry.

Flaps Getting his first stripe up! Big moment that is. Lance Bombardier.

Maggie Yes. Great isn't it?

Sophie I'm so sorry, Mags. I assumed you knew.

Sal Maybe he was keeping it as a surprise.

Sophie Sorry. Me and my big mouth.

Tom (*taking Harry to one side*) Sorry to tell you this, Harry, but I suspect we've lost Jacko.

Sophie No!

Harry What? Permanently? Why?

Tom He . . . (*Not sure how to tell him.*) He's –

Harry Oh no. What's happened?

Tom Not good.

Harry What?

Tom Caught shop lifting. DVDs you apparently told him to get.

Harry Look at, not steal!

Harry turns to go upstage. Suddenly Woody has come back into the rehearsal room. He grabs Harry from behind. Around his neck. There's a lot of screaming and panic. All the dialogue overlaps.

Sophie Woody! What the fuck?!

Flaps What are you doing?

Rickshaw Christ!

Flaps Alright mate. Calm / down.

Rickshaw What the fuck?!

Tom Woody, you're a Marine, behave like a / Marine –

Woody Or what? You'll beat me with your stick, 'sir'?! And officially, from the 23rd I'm not a Royal Marine Commando. But who gives a shit? No one noticed. Nobody cared. Do you know what happened the morning I left. I handed in my kit. I thought there'd be a 'Good bye Woody. Thanks for helping us out with all that killing and stuff.' Nothing. I was brushed aside with the empties. The last thing I had to do was hand in my pass at the gate. I stood there, thinking the guy might say something. Anything. But no. He just looks at me, says 'What the fuck are you still doing here?' Foxtrot Oscar. Is that what you want me to do? Foxtrot Oscar?! It's bullshit. This outpouring of stories can rescue us bullshit. This isn't going to bring back my mate Bagsy.

Harry I know.

Woody You don't fucking know. Unless you've been there. What fear is. And looks like and smells like.

Len I do, Woody. I do. But it's not their fault.

Woody I didn't say it was.

Flaps Then why do *this*?!

Woody I killed people. Husbands and wives. I fucking killed them and they hadn't done anything to me. I took their lives. With steel and fire and biblical wrath. How do you show them that? That gristle in your teeth of what war is?

Flaps We don't. That's why / we are –

Rickshaw (*ashamed and angry*) We were doing the job, Wood. That's all.

Woody That's all. Doing the job. What a fucking job. (*His head is a mass of noise and voices. To the women and Harry.*) Understand what it feels like now, do you? Feel it? Smell it? Is that authentic enough for you?

Woody releases Harry who holds his throat, in shock. No one quite knows what to do. Len starts to go.

Woody Where are you going, Lenny?

Len Call the police.

Sal No. Wait.

Len I have to call the police.

Sal They'll bang him up.

Len There's been an assault.

Harry Len! Wait.

Tom No, Harry. Not this time.

Harry Look! Stop. Please. (*Clutching at straws*) I'm sorry.

This confounds all of them.

Tom What?

Beth Why are *you* sorry?

Harry Okay. Look. (*Thinking fast.*) Woody was right. Okay. (*To Woody.*) You were right. He was right.

Tom What the hell are you talking about?

The others are perplexed. Even Woody seems surprised.

Harry He said that's what would happen.

Maggie What would happen?

There is now real confusion.

Harry If he did that. Didn't you? Woody?

Sophie I don't understand?

Sal (*to Harry*) Did you plan this?

Trees (*to Woody*) You threatened us and you planned it?

Beth What kind of sick mind does that?

Maggie I hope you're proud of yourself.

Harry (*taking the flack*) It's completely my fault. The exercise had to be real. To understand. Otherwise it would all have / been –

Maggie (*appalled*) You can't do that to people.

Tom I really don't approve of that, Harry.

Harry I know.

Tom I'm sorry but that's going way beyond / the –

Harry I know. I'm sorry. I'm sorry everyone. (*Turns to Woody.*) I'm sorry, Woody.

Tom Christ.

Everyone melts away from the stage, except Harry and Woody, who advances on Harry and stands very close to him.

Woody What did you say that for?

No reply.

Huh? Fuck you. I didn't ask you to do that. Save my arse.

He starts to go, stops, turns around and comes back and hugs Harry. But Harry does not reciprocate. He just stands there.

By the way, did I mention I'm fucked up.

He smiles at Harry, pats him on the arm and starts to go.

Harry You're not a soldier any more, Woody. Don't be a victim.

This stops Woody in his tracks. He considers this, then goes.

TWELVE
AWOL

Jacko is packing his small bag. Harry stands in the doorway, watching him.

Harry How did they catch you?

Jacko (*stops packing for a moment, thinks*) Cos I was a bit rusty, I s'pose. Never used to have a problem nicking DVDs from there before. (*Packing.*) Did it hundreds of times.

Harry Why didn't you ask me?

Jacko Ask you for what?

Harry Help?

Jacko What? Nicking DVDs?

Harry Don't be flippant.

Jacko stops packing and looks at Harry. Then turns back and carries on packing.

Jacko Right.

Harry I could have leant you the films. Money.

Jacko Don't want to do that, sir.

Harry You didn't have to go and start nicking.

Jacko (*smiles to himself*) Right. What was the ppppoint thinking I could have been an actor, eh? That was never going to happen in a million years.

Harry Yes it could. Why not?

Jacko (*stops packing*) Someone like me? I'm damned. Damned if I do, damned if I don't.

Harry No. Jacko, no.

Jacko I've done terrible things, do you know that? Bbbeen told it makes it alright bbbb bbbecause it was for Queen and Country and all that . . . Bbbut I come home, and I'm thinking . . . I did my job, and I try and sleep at night –

He takes his time over the word 'but' as he doesn't want to stutter, and breathes deliberately.

But the demons are waiting for me. They're always waiting for me. Under that bed. Or another bed. And no one really wants to know about what happened. What we did. Not really.

Harry I do. The play does.

Jacko Not really.

Harry Where are you going?

Jacko I'm not allowed to stay here any more. Bbbbroke the rules . . . So I'm between places right now.

Harry (*getting out his wallet*) Look, let me lend you a few quid.

Jacko No, mate. (*Shakes his head.*) Don't bother. I'll get by. Got my pension due at the end of the month. I'll kip over at a mate's.

Harry We need you.

Jacko No you don't.

Harry I'm sorry, Jacko.

Jacko That's real life for you. Always getting in the way. Biting you on the bum.

Harry I thought I could help.

Jacko Your type always does.

Harry My type?

Jacko Empathetic . . . but not really brave enough to . . .

Harry To what?

Jacko No. I know you mean well. (*Beat.*) Not *Soldier, Soldier*, though is it?

    Harry doesn't respond.

No happy endings.

Harry I was sacked from *Soldier, Soldier*.

Jacko Why?

Harry Lost my nerve. Bottled it.

Jacko How's that?

Harry Couldn't remember the lines. When it mattered. I'd go blank as soon as I heard the word 'action'.

Jacko Fuck.

Harry Yeah. Oh, the producer was sympathetic. Saw a shrink. Did aromatherapy. Didn't work.

Jacko So you thought you'd give directing a go.

Harry Something like that. It was the last bit of acting I did.

You sure about that?

He has seen through Harry, who nods and starts packing again.

Harry Seriously? Is that what you think I've been doing? (*Beat.*) I just want to give something back, Jacko.

Jacko Why?

Harry You may think I don't understand. And maybe I don't. What happened to you. (Thinks before sharing.) My brother took his life. Long time ago. Still hurts, and I still wish I could have done more.

Jacko now understands Harry a lot more.

So, yes I care, okay.

Jacko Good luck with that, sir.

He takes his case. Harry's voice stops him at the door.

Harry Jacko, if you think you can, you can. If you think you can't –

Jacko You can't. Either way you're right. Henry Ford. ('*I'm not some dumb squaddie.*') Way ahead of you, sir.

Harry Which mate?

Jacko What?

Harry Which mate are you going to stay with?

Jacko smiles. He gets lost in the crowd. A phone rings.

Blackout.

TC stands on one side of the stage, looking out at the audience.

   Sonya (Tanya) enters and stands on the other side of the stage.

Sonya Hello? Sonya speaking. (*No reply.*) Hello? Who is this? (*Beat. She knows who it is.*) Why do you keep doing this? What do you want? (*No reply.*) I don't know what you want?

TC turns to face Sonya. Desperate to say something, but he can't get the words out.

Darren (*James, voice from off*) Mum?

Sonya (*to the offstage voice*) I'm coming. (*To the audience/phone.*) Is that you, TC?

TC freezes.

You can't keep doing this, Terry. Do you understand? Just to hear my voice. It's not healthy.

TC is in mental torment.

Where are you? Are you okay? Where are you living?

No reply

Sonya (*kind, but spelling it out*) You can come home any time, you do understand that, don't you? It's up to you. What you do. No one's stopping you be here. Just you. We're here, Terrence. We miss you. Come home, love.

TC turns away from Sonya, and this signals that he has put the phone down on her.

Darren (*voice from off*) Who was that, Mum?

Sonya (*thinks for a moment*) It was that PPI again.

Darren (*voice from off*) Just block the number, Mum.

Sonya is in torment. She misses TC.

THIRTEEN
MISFIRE

The actors are doing a bit from the boot dance routine. There is no Woody or Jacko. Beth misses the synch on the final beat and lands a beat after everyone else.

Beth Oh fuck it! Fuck, fuck, FUCK!

Harry comes onto the stage. He has his script.

Harry It's okay. We've still got the dress rehearsal.

Flaps It's every bloody time.

Beth Oi! Oi! Wind your fucking neck in, you!

Maggie Bethany!

Beth People in glass houses, mate! (*To Rickshaw.*) And you, Rickshaw! Rickerfuckingmortis!

Harry Alright. Alright!

Len (*coming on from the auditorium*) Oi! That's enough. All of you.

Sophie But basically that's where James Blunt takes over?

Harry He's not taking over.

Sophie But that's where he'll come on.

Rickshaw While we stand around like spare pricks till he's done?

Harry Not spare pricks, Rickshaw, no. (*Hoping Len will say something positive.*) Len, what do you think?

The look on Len's face says 'car crash'.

Len Well . . . It was, um . . . I mean there were several bits that were . . . no, it were fucking awful, Harry. You can't put that on stage, not with our name all over it.

Jenny Now wait just a minute.

Len Sal!

Sal What?

Len You've got to be louder. (*To Tanya and Jenny.*) So have you two. (*To Jenny.*) And you – they, Jenny, whatever – your face needs more expressions.

Jenny What?!

Len And Hoarse, you've got to get on top of them lines, you're way off the pace pal. Sophie, you've got to be more – (*Makes a gesture with his hands, shaking some invisible sholuders.*) You know.

Sophie No, I don't know.

Len Yes, you do. More – (*Makes the same gesture again.*)

Sophie What's? (*She copies Len's shaking gesture with her hands.*)

Len Exactly. And Rickshaw you've got to drive those scenes, mate.

Rickshaw Drive what?

Len You heard. He's told you enough times. He's angry. And Flaps, you've got to be funnier, lad. He's written you funny lines, but your timing's all wrong. Beth – (*Shakes* *his head.*) I don't know where to begin with you kid . . . you look like you've got two left feet love.

Beth Charming –

Len And Trees, you've got Asperger's, love, not depression.

Maggie Have you finished, Len?

Len It's like the platoon, you've all got to become bigger than the sum of your parts.

Maggie And what about me then?

Len You? Oh no, you were great.

Sophie Harry?

Harry What Len said.

Sophie Look. We're papering over cracks, Harry. It just doesn't work any more.

Sal No, it doesn't.

Trees We have tried, Harry.

Sophie But without Jacko –

Flaps Or Woody –

Sophie It doesn't work. It just doesn't.

Harry Okay, well, that means more cuts.

Sal NO! (*To Len.*) Loud enough for you?!

Tanya We can't take more cuts!

Harry Tom?

Tom (*off*) Yeah?

Harry Can you bring the prompt copy?

Sophie But you've already slashed it to pieces.

Harry (*angry*) What else am I meant to do? I lost half the cast.

Sophie bursts into tears and walks away from Harry.

Rickshaw (*going to Sophie*) Thanks a bunch.

Harry throws down his file.

Jenny Oops. File down again.

Tom comes on.

Tom (*going over to Harry and pushing the prompt copy at him him*) Bloody shower!

He walks off.

Harry We're short. We're short.

He knows this is going to be a long shot. He calls to the back of the auditorium.

TC ? You up there TC?

TC (*comes up from upstage behind Harry*) Yes, boss? Sound okay?

Harry It's great, TC.

TC Thank you.

Harry just looks at TC. And TC knows exactly what Harry is going to ask him.

TC (*his face falls*) No. I'm sorry but the answer's no, Harry.

Beth Why not?

TC I said. Right at the start.

Harry But –

TC I can't. Okay. I just can't.

Tanya You're the only other person who knows the show, TC.

TC Len can do it. (*He rushes offstage.*)

Everyone looks at Len.

Sophie Len *can* do it.

Sal You'll be great Len. You know all the letters.

Sophie You would, Len. We'll go through all the Donny stuff till your . . . (*She does the shaking gesture with her hands again.*)

Rickshaw Come on, Len. Put your money where your mouth is.

Maggie (*flirty but not about to take no for an answer*) Please, Len. We're desperate.

Len (*tentative*) Oh, alright then.

Rickshaw But we haven't got Woody, we're still short.

Jenny (*comes forward, and is unusually confident*) You do it then, Harry.

Harry Me? No.

Beth You could go on with a script.

Harry No. Absolutely not.

Sophie You know it, Harry,

Flaps You wrote the bloody thing!

Harry I said no.

Jenny You don't need the script.

Harry I can't.

Sal Please, Harry.

Rickshaw Please.

Maggie Please.

They all start chanting 'Harry'. Under the weight of the requests Harry storms off. The others look at each other. Then follow him.

FOURTEEN
FIGHT OR FLIGHT

Len goes off to find Harry.

Len Harry? (*No reply.*) Harry?

Harry I've really ballsed this thing up, haven't I?

Len (*thinks*) Yup.

Harry Can't you even lie a bit to make me feel better?!

Len We haven't got time for you to have a meltdown as well. There's a queue. (*Silence.*) Look, when you came to us with the idea of doing a play –

Harry I know. You hated it.

Len When you were in *Soldier, Soldier*, you came and filmed at our barracks.

Harry Oh dear. Really? I hope you weren't scarred for life.

Len You were very kind.

Harry Was I?

Len Yes. You signed my box set of Series 6.

Harry I didn't know you cared.

Len Not for me, you daft twat. It was for my wife, Jess. She was a big fan.

Harry Oh.

Len Not you. Robson and Jerome.

Harry Right.

Len She was much more creative than I was. She'll be having a right old laugh if she knew I were going to be doing a play. (*Talks to the heavens.*) I'm doing a play Jess . . . (*To Harry.*) That's why I keep the bees. She asked me to. Before she died. She said I needed something creative in my life. I poo-pooed it at the time, but after a while I thought . . . well, I didn't have anything else going on, we couldn't have kids, so I bought a couple of hives. Best thing I ever did . . . until this . . . now.

Harry turns to look at Len.

Look, I don't know. But, we've come this far. Haven't we?

Harry I can't do it Len. Don't you understand? (*Ashamed.*) I've got stage fright.

Len (*not quite sure what to say back*) You think we haven't?! What about being in the arena, Harry? Daring greatly. Was that all bollocks then? They're all facing their fears, and bloody doing it. And me.

He walks off.

FIFTEEN
GOING OVER THE TOP

In the green room, backstage. The actors are all coming in. There are last-minute adjustments to the costumes and putting boots on. We hear the sound of the audience over the Tannoy, then hear Tom over the Tannoy.

Tom (*voice-over*) Ladies and gentlemen of the 'Soldier On Company', this is your five-minute call. You have five minutes please.

Beth (*pacing up and down*) Oh God, oh God, oh God, oh God.

Rickshaw What are you worried about? I thought you played the Albert Hall.

Flaps And Wembley Stadium.

Beth That's singing, mate. I've got bloody lines in this! Loads of them. 'Tip of the tongue, top of the teeth. Tip of the tongue, top of the teeth.'

Rickshaw (*copying and taking the mick*) 'Top of the clock, base of the cock. Top of the clock, base of the cock.'

Beth Oh shut up. Feels like we're about to go over the top.

Rickshaw Well you are. You always are.

TC comes on and puts a radio mic on Rickshaw.

Beth Swear to God I'll bloody slam you one of these days. (*Holding out her fist to him.*)

Rickshaw Now you're just flirting!

Beth And it was Twickenham, not Wembley.

Maggie (*entering, putting on lipstick*) Right. Are we all set?

Sophie (*entering*) We all look like we're from North fucking Korea!!

Tanya (*coming on, in a panic*) Hair up or down, TC? TC?

No, I always have it down.

Tanya hits TC playfully. Hoarse comes on. Panicked.

Hoarse Someone needs to fix that bloody lock, it could have been dangerous.

TC Wear it up. It suits you up.

Tanya smiles and TC smiles back.
Len comes on. He is also in his green boiler suit and boots.

Len Right. How do I look?

Maggie Very becoming.

Flaps You scrubbed up alright.

Len Thanks very much.

Flaps Not you, you daft bugger.

They all make last-minute adjustments. Maggie adjusts Tom's boiler suit.

Flaps Oi, Trees? Do you think I *could* be funnier?

Trees Yes.

Flaps (*disappointed*) Oh. Right.

Trees Fancy coming up to Bonfire's Point later?

Flaps Yeah? Yeah. I'd like that. We can do a bit of –

Trees (*smiling*) Screaming? –

Flaps Dogging.

She hits him playfully.

And screaming.

Hoarse goes over to Jenny. She isn't sure what he's going to do.

Jenny (*wary*) What?

Hoarse Nothing. Just thought I'd say good luck, that's all.

Jenny (*not quite sure what to do with that remark*) Right. Thank you. And you.

107

Hoarse (*gives Jenny a pair of earrings*) These belonged to my ex. I thought they might suit you.

Jenny Thank you. Earrings. You won't be needing them then? On exercise?

Hoarse Nah. Not my colour.

Jenny goes off, trying on an earring, passing Harry entering in boiler suit and boots.

Sophie What is it, Harry?

Harry Look, um, there's good news and there's some bad news. The bad news is . . . I'm afraid James Blunt isn't going to be able to get here tonight.

Beth What?!

Rickshaw So, how's that bad news then?

Tanya Oh, shut up!

Harry He's sent us this. (*He reads the email.*) But the good news is . . .

He turns to the wings and on comes Jacko, in his green boiler suit. Sophie is so pleased to see him she gives him a huge hug.

Jacko I'm back. Easy.

Sophie Thank you.

Flaps Typical Paras. Always late and never there when you need them.

Jacko Oi!

Sophie Oh yes they are. (*She's so pleased to see Jacko.*)

Harry So back to Plan A everyone. With the exception of Woody.

Jacko I tried to find him. But I don't think he wants to be found.

Harry Well, let's see how well I actually do know this script then.

Tom appears.

Tom Okay, ladies and gentlemen of the 'Soldier On Company', this is it - your beginners' call.

There is an anxious but excited reaction.

Tom Everyone got props? Right. It's a pretty full house, so . . . Remember the old army adage: 'Bullshit baffles brains'. (*They all laugh.*) Now, would you all please make your way to the stage for the top of Act One. This is your beginners' call.

They all start to make their way off. Harry stops them.

Harry I just wanted to say . . . what a pleasure it has been to work with you all.

Jacko laughs.

Not you. (*He gets out a piece of paper.*) And I found this . . . (*Unfolds the paper and reads.*) 'Things can be salvaged in stories. And by passing these stories on – we keep the past alive. Otherwise history is left to rust, if it weren't for the outstretched hand of . . . "Once upon a time".' (*Beat. He folds the paper and thinks about what he is going to say next.*) We learn from these stories . . . we honour them. Give them meaning. (*Beat.*) Go out there, enjoy yourselves. It doesn't matter what comes out the other end. As my old friend the Scottish king said . . .

Rickshaw Told you he was posh.

Harry 'Be bloody, bold and resolute.' To absent friends.

All Absent friends.

Impromptu, they all put their right hands into the middle and join them together, and look at each other. They say 'Absent friends'. As they take their hands away and move off, Harry sees that Tom didn't quite make it into the huddle. He does another bringing of hands together with just Tom. They then go.

Maggie stops in her tracks. Cameron stands opposite her. He is dressed in a suit.

Cameron Hiya. You look great, Mum.

Maggie (*beat, not quite sure what to say*) Thank you.

Cameron Wouldn't have missed it.

Maggie and Cameron I'm sorry.

Maggie You're not supposed to see me now. We're about to go on.

Chrissy suddenly comes on, looking for Cameron.

Chrissy We've got to get to our seats, Cam.

She sees Maggie. There is moment between all three of them.

Cameron We'll see you after, then? We can give you a wave.

Maggie Don't you dare. You'll put me right off.

Cameron Okay. (*Gives her a kiss.*)

Chrissy Break a leg. That's what they say, isn't it?

Maggie (*nods and smiles*) You better go.

Chrissy takes Cam's hand and goes. Maggie watches them.

Maggie Lance Bombardier.

This stops him. He turns, smiles and nods at her, she smiles back, and he goes. A figure in the shadows stops Maggie.

Paula Excuse me?

Maggie Can I help you? You watching, luv?

Paula I am. Yeah.

Maggie You better hurry up. We're about to start.

Paula Can you just give this to Sean?

Maggie Sorry, who?

Paula Sean? Oh, Rickshaw

She hands Maggie an old straw hat.

Maggie He'll know what it's about?

Paula (*nods*) Yeah. He'll know.

There is a moment of recognition between them of sacrifice and understanding.

Blackout.

SIXTEEN

THEATRE OF WAR . . . DARING GREATLY

As per the start of the show. The lights come up on . . . Harry, alone, feeling the fear, but somehow doing it anyway.

Harry Many years passed. And the dragon had gone to live all alone in a cave at the edge of the sea. But he saw other dragons that had become frozen in the ice, which scared him even more. (*Losing confidence.*) And he tried . . . he tried to drown himself in the sea and make it go away . . . make it all go away.

Jacko (*coming across to Harry and putting a kindly hand on his shoulder*) Until, one day, Ryan forgot how to breathe this fire. He began to breathe hot air again. And he realised he could use this hot air for good. There were qualities he'd forgotten he had. He could fly.

Tom And what an amazing thing that was . . . to be able to fly.

Harry stands in the middle, becoming surrounded by his actors. They come onto the stage when they add their line. It's underscored by Tine Thing Helseth's trumpet arrangement of Rachmaninov's 'Zdes' Khorosho', which plays right through till Rickshaw's final speech.

Sophie And news went out across the land – a little boy and his sister were lost . . .

Sal And Ryan flew off into the night sky and he found them. He rescued them, and he took them home.

Everyone Thank you. Thank you. Everyone said.

Maggie And soon other people were coming to see the dragon and asking for his help.

Trees He found that he was useful again.

Len 'Please help us fly off into the sky. To be on top of the world. To see the world anew,' they said.

Flaps Until one day the Prince, and Princess, were on the path atop the very sea, and the very cave where the dragon lived.

Beth And when they saw him blowing hot air into huge balloons, they were amazed.

Jenny Great big balloons, that would have huge baskets attached.

Everyone The dragon that could help people fly.

Hoarse And they got in the balloon.

They all correct him: 'Basket!'

Hoarse Basket.

TC And he blew the biggest, warmest breath that he could make.

Everyone And the balloon began to rise. And rise. And rise.

Rickshaw And the dragon smiled and was happy at last.

Tanya 'Thank you, dragon. This is for you,' they said.

Sal He held out his hand –

Woody And he held out his hand, and they threw down the crown.

They are all surprised to see Woody and turn to look at him as he comes on. He throws the straw hat down in front of Rickshaw and Sal.

Rickshaw Which the dragon wore for the rest of his life.

Sal puts the hat on Rickshaw's head and smartens him up.

And who knows . . . he may still be there for all I know.

The music ends. Woody walks forward.

Woody And that, ladies and gentlemen, was the birth of Ryan Air.

They all shout 'WOODY!!'

Woody WHAT?!

Len (*barking an order*) Company! Company, shun!

They all come to attention in their opening positions and the music starts for 'Carry You Home' by Ward Thomas. They sing and dance one final time as they take their bows.

Soldier On Anthem Reprise

When the dark descends on you.
And a smile hides despair.
When the lights don't shine on you,
And it all feels unfair.

When it's all too much for you,
And no one is there.
When the world's lost touch with you,
And it's too much to bear.

We will endeavour to
Turn back the tide.
With heads together, we'll
Be right by your side.

We will be there for you,
To catch you if you fall.
Shine a light if it's dark for you,
All for one and one for all.

Let go of yesterday,
Of all the things you've seen and done.
Let go what others say,
And together, we will, Soldier On.

Let go of yesterday,
Of all the things you've seen and done.
Let go what others say,
And together, we will, Soldier On.